"I can't go to your apartment," Christy said. "I'll get a hotel room."

"The hell you will. There's somebody out there who's after you. If he can get to you here, he can get to you in a hotel. No. You're coming to my apartment."

"And why can't he get to me at your apartment?"

"Besides the fact that there's a security guard on duty 24/7? And it's on the eighth floor? Because I'll be there."

"No." She shook her head. "I can't."

"I don't see why not. Get packed."

"Because—" She stopped. She couldn't tell him why she didn't want to stay with him. She wasn't sure she could explain it to herself. She'd like to think it was because he was overprotective, bossy.

But that wasn't it.

She could get used to having a knight in shining armor around.

MALLORY KANE

THE PEDIATRICIAN'S PERSONAL PROTECTOR

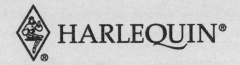 **HARLEQUIN®**

TORONTO • NEW YORK • LONDON
AMSTERDAM • PARIS • SYDNEY • HAMBURG
STOCKHOLM • ATHENS • TOKYO • MILAN • MADRID
PRAGUE • WARSAW • BUDAPEST • AUCKLAND

To Daddy, my hero and my biggest fan.
I know you and Mama are dancing.

Recycling programs
for this product may
not exist in your area.

ISBN-13: 978-0-373-69510-2

THE PEDIATRICIAN'S PERSONAL PROTECTOR

ABOUT THE AUTHOR

Mallory has two very good reasons for loving reading and writing. Her mother was a librarian, who taught her to love and respect books as a precious resource. Her father could hold listeners spellbound for hours with his stories. He was always her biggest fan.

Mallory loves romantic suspense with dangerous heroes and dauntless heroines, and enjoys tossing in a bit of her medical knowledge for an extra dose of intrigue. Mallory lives in Mississippi with her computer-genius husband and three exceptionally intelligent cats.

She enjoys hearing from readers. You can write her at mallory@mallorykane.com or via Harlequin Books.

Books by Mallory Kane

†Black Hills Brotherhood
*The Delancey Dynasty

CAST OF CHARACTERS

Reilly Delancey—A top SWAT sniper and hostage negotiator, Reilly has a knack for getting at the truth.

Christy Moser—Christy longs to confide in police officer Reilly Delancey, but he wears a badge. And she believes the police are responsible for taking away everyone she loved.

Ryker Delancey—Reilly needs his twin brother to give him vital information about his fellow detectives. But when the chips are down, will his brother's loyalty to the badge prove stronger than blood?

Charles Phillips—The veteran detective is overweight and lumbering, but has never had a black mark on his record and he's close to retirement. There's no way he'd jeopardize his pension, right?

Ted Dagewood—The big, good-looking police detective is obnoxious and arrogant, and he's been known to rough up a suspect to get what he wants. But he's a good cop, isn't he?

Bill Crenshaw—Reilly's brother, Ryker's, friend and fellow detective may have a confidential informant whose fingerprints are on the gun that killed Christy's sister. But Ryker swears his friend isn't involved.

Chapter One

Reilly Delancey was late. He hurried up the steps of the St. Tammany Parish courthouse, through the metal detectors and into the large central hall, fingering the knot of his tie and wishing he hadn't tied it so tightly.

He spoke to a couple of fellow officers who were waiting to testify in other cases. They had the same resigned expression on their faces that he was sure was on his.

A quick glance at the courtroom schedule told him that the McGilicutty case, in which he was testifying as the lead hostage negotiator, was in Courtroom Three. He rushed to the door, only to be stopped by the assistant district attorney who'd prepped him.

"Judge Simmons just got here," Hale Dunham told him. "It'll be at least twenty minutes before we need you."

"Simmons is hearing the case? It'll be thirty. I'll get a cup of coffee."

"Be back in fifteen," Hale warned.

"Eighteen," he countered and headed toward the small kiosk on the far side of the hall. If Simmons had just entered the courtroom, it would be ten minutes before he finished straightening his robes and arranging his gavel and pens. Then another twenty before the preliminaries were over. Simmons questioned everything.

He ordered and paid for his coffee and dumped sugar into

it, then stood sipping it as he glanced around at the hubbub in the courthouse.

Two detectives walked by. Dagewood and Phillips. He didn't remember their first names. They worked with his twin brother, Detective Ryker Delancey. Phillips was loud and overweight, but basically he seemed like a good guy. Dagewood, on the other hand, was arrogant and rude.

As if to prove Reilly's opinion, Dagewood stopped in front of him. "Well," he said. "If it's not the Delancey that *didn't* make detective."

Reilly bit his tongue. Somehow, Dagewood had figured out how badly Reilly had coveted the position Ryker had gotten, and he mentioned it every chance he got.

"Dagewood," Reilly responded noncommittally, taking his own shot. The big detective liked the uniformed officers to address him by his title, so Reilly never did.

"So what's up today?" Dagewood continued. "Defending a traffic ticket?"

Phillips chuckled at the old joke.

Reilly sipped his coffee and didn't answer.

"Come on, Ted," Phillips said. "I didn't get any breakfast. By the time we get back to the office, all the doughnuts'll be gone."

"Hang on," Dagewood said. "I haven't tried the coffee here. If it's good enough for Delancey..."

Phillips laughed again and the two stood in line.

Reilly ignored them as his gaze slid over the crowd. He half expected to see Ryker. His brother was here for the sentencing hearing of the man who'd killed four women in St. Tammany Parish over the past five years.

Reilly and Ryker didn't normally see each other a lot these days. They ran in different circles since Ryker was a detective and Reilly was SWAT. But Reilly had babysat his brother's injured star witness a few weeks ago while Ryker was booking the killer. She wasn't just his star witness either. Since two weeks ago, she was his fiancée.

Ryker engaged. Reilly shook his head. Hard to believe. Before his older brother—older by seven minutes—had met Nicole Beckham, he'd never even dated anyone seriously.

As his thoughts wandered and his coffee cooled, his gaze settled on what just might be the most striking woman he'd ever seen. She was tall and slender, with midnight-black hair that fell to her shoulders and a confident walk that had more eyes than his following her.

As soon as he realized that most of the males in the central hall were watching her, it became obvious that she wasn't paying attention to any of them. She was headed straight for him.

Or more likely, for the coffee kiosk.

Whatever she had her eyes on, Reilly would bet a month's pay that she'd get it. She was the confident, super-cool type who got whatever she wanted. He swallowed a chuckle as he watched her mow down the men in her path with a glare. Her high heels clicked with purpose on the marble floor.

He couldn't tell where she was looking behind the narrow, black-rimmed glasses she wore, but he managed to resist the urge to glance behind him. He kept his gaze on her face. He was dying to know if her eyes were as black as her hair and her glasses frames. He got his answer when she stopped directly in front of him.

They weren't black. They were green. And flashing with irritation. At him.

At him?

"Detective Delancey," she said, propping a hand on her hip.

Reilly shook his head and muttered his automatic response. "No, I'm not—"

"Don't start with me again, Detective. You must be so

proud. My father is barely recovered from the heart attack he suffered in *your* jail less than two weeks ago. But he was determined to stand before the judge and plead guilty. How could you be so quick to catch him, but no one can find my sister's killer? Why don't you spend some time on that!" She paused to take a breath.

Reilly jumped at the opportunity. "I'm not Detective Delancey," he said quickly. "People make that mistake all the time. I'm—"

She jerked off her glasses and took aim with those laser-sharp eyes. "What do you mean you're not—" She stopped, frowning at him.

Reilly assessed her more closely as, behind him, Phillips chuckled. Then Dagewood spoke up loudly. "Need any help there, *Officer* Delancey?"

Without the glasses shielding her eyes, he could see something behind their cool expression. Something that was far from cool and far from confident. The lids were rimmed with red and faintly puffy. Her generous mouth was pressed into a severe line, and the skin along her jawline appeared stretched tight. He could see pale blue veins under the delicate skin of her neck. The black-haired beauty was wound tight as a spring about to break.

He replayed her words in his mind, fitting the pieces together.

Detective Delancey—

My father...pleaded guilty—

She was the daughter of Ryker's serial killer. That surprised him. He wracked his brain, but couldn't come up with the man's name.

"No. You're not Detective Delancey," she said, shaking her head.

He shrugged, intrigued that she'd arrived at that conclusion so quickly. Usually it was the other way around. He'd had people actually argue with him about which twin he was, and so had Ryker. Which was funny, because he didn't think he and his brother were alike at all. Both of them had always been lean, but Ryker had put on a little weight in the past year. And Reilly was a lot less OCD about haircuts and clothes and life in general.

"Sorry," he said to the woman. "It happens a lot. Especially if I'm dressed up." He ran his finger under his collar again. "Which is as seldom as possible. I hate suits."

The tension around her mouth softened a bit.

"I'm Officer Reilly Delancey. SWAT." He held out his hand.

From behind him he heard, "The Delancey that didn't make detective," followed by Phillips's annoying laugh. One day he was going to punch Dagewood.

She ignored or didn't notice his hand as she sent a swift, withering glance toward the two detectives. "Where is Detective Delancey?" she asked, looking at her watch. "He disappeared as soon as the judge dismissed us. I thought maybe he'd be out here."

"My guess is, if he's not scheduled for another court appearance, he's gone to check on his fiancée," Reilly replied.

The woman in front of him stiffened even more.

"To check on his fiancée? Of course. That's exactly what I'd do after I put a sick old man in prison. Or maybe I'd go to Disney World."

Reilly's hackles rose at her sarcasm, although he could hardly blame her for being upset. After all, she'd just witnessed her father plead guilty to what—four counts of murder? Still, he leaped to his brother's defense, choosing his next words carefully.

"My brother's fiancée was injured on the day your father was arrested," he said carefully. "She had a doctor's appointment this morning."

Her sharp glance and the grimace of pain that passed fleetingly across her face told him she understood what he hadn't said. Ryker's fiancée's injury had been at her father's hand.

"I'm sorry about your father—and your sister," he offered.

Her mouth tightened. "Why?" she asked. "You don't know me. Or my family."

"I know a little about your father's case. How the death of your sister—"

"How can I find Detective Delancey?" she interrupted, two bright spots of color appearing in her pale cheeks.

Despite her words, what he heard was *that's none of your business.* And it wasn't. He'd crossed a line. He immediately backtracked.

"He's probably already left the courthouse. If you want, I can make sure he gets in touch with you."

She glanced at her watch, then back at Reilly. Suddenly she appeared unsure, and that surprised him. She didn't seem like the type to ever be unsure of anything. She might be wrong, as she was in thinking he was Ryker, but she would always be sure.

"Hand me your phone," he said.

She put her glasses back on and gave him a narrow look. For a moment he wasn't sure she was going to comply. But finally her hand snaked inside her purse and she handed him a smart phone. He quickly programmed his number and name into it, then pressed Call. His cell phone began to ring. He dug it out of his pocket, answered it, then hung up her phone and handed it back to her.

"What's your name?" he asked without looking up.

"Dr. Moser," she said without hesitation.

He raised his gaze to hers.

"Christy—Moser." She stared for an instant at the display

on her smart phone, then stuck it into the pocket of her jacket.

Reilly finished entering her name into his phone. "Okay. I'll get my brother to call you."

"How soon? I need to find out what happens next. How long my father has before he—" She stopped and cleared her throat. "I have to go," she said. She fingered the watch on her left wrist and looked at it for the third time. Or was it the fourth?

"Yeah, me too," he said, checking the time on his phone's display before he pocketed it. His seventeen minutes were up. He had to get to Courtroom Three.

Christy Moser turned and walked away. Reilly watched her excellent backside sway in the black fitted skirt. It was amazing how high-heeled shoes affected a woman's walk. In a good way.

Dr. Moser. He'd have to ask Ryker what kind of doctor the serial killer's daughter was.

CHRISTMAS LEIGH MOSER stood at the front door of the house where she and her sister Autumn had grown up in Covington, Louisiana. Yellow crime-scene tape crisscrossed the door-frame, garish against the dingy white paint.

She stared at it, aghast. Why was her dad's house a crime scene? Nothing Detective Delancey had told her had indicated that her father had done anything here. Horror churned in her stomach, mingled with shame.

She hadn't been in the house since her sister's death. She should have made more of an effort to get back here to see her dad. But two years of residency plus a fellowship in pediatrics at one of the foremost children's hospitals in the northeast made it difficult to get home to sleep, much less take a trip thirteen hundred miles away.

She'd called him every week—well, nearly every week.

How had she not known something was dreadfully wrong with him? How had she not realized he'd gone off the deep end?

A twinge under her breastbone gave her the answer to that. She *had* known something was wrong. Known it and ignored it. She'd chalked up his monotone answers and disinterest to mild situational depression, and had encouraged him to get out more, see his friends, get back to playing golf. She'd told him he should talk to someone and suggested that he ask the pastor of his church about a grief-counseling class or a therapist.

She thought about the one time she had visited her dad in the past five years. She'd attended a seminar in New Orleans. She'd met her dad at a restaurant for a hurried dinner before kissing him on the cheek and rushing back to her hotel room to prepare for a talk she was giving the next day.

Now here she was. Too late. Her family home had become the home of a killer.

She shuddered, swallowing hard. Shock and revulsion and fear had dogged her steps ever since she'd received the phone call telling her that her father had been arrested. The call had come less than twelve hours after she'd talked to her dad. When she put the times together, she realized that within an hour of their conversation, he'd shot two people, a policeman and a restaurant owner, and had tried to kill a third.

He'd done it with the misguided notion that he could force the police to reopen Autumn's case.

Guilt washed over Christy like a blast of hot summer wind, stealing her breath and leaving her back and neck prickling with sudden sweat. The certainty that this was her fault sat like a dead weight on her chest. She'd gone off and left him to deal with Autumn, knowing her younger sister was in trouble with drugs.

If she'd stayed in Louisiana, would her little sister still be alive? Would her father be an active, vibrant man in his early sixties, rather than a deranged murderer?

Rationally, she recognized that her decision probably wouldn't have changed what happened, but rationality and guilt were like matter and antimatter. They couldn't occupy the same space. And the guilt was stronger.

Christy realized she'd become exactly what she'd sworn she'd never be, a workaholic career woman with no time for family, like her mother. Deborah Moser had been a tenured professor at Loyola until the day she'd been in the wrong place at the wrong time.

Christy glanced around the neighborhood where she and Autumn had played as children. None of the neighbors were outside, and there were no cars on the street. She'd once known many of the people who lived here. Where were they now? Resentment burned deep within her. Why hadn't they known something was wrong with her dad?

Why hadn't she?

She looked down at the key in her hand. Suddenly, she needed to go inside and look at her father's things. See her sister's room. Wallow in some more guilt.

She slipped the key into the lock and turned it. The door opened easily, silently.

Christy ducked under the crime-scene tape. She pushed the door wide. The first thing that struck her was how dark the inside of the house was. The second, that it had been that way ever since their mother had been killed when Christy was sixteen and Autumn was twelve.

Leaving the front door open for light, she stepped over to her father's recliner and turned on the lamp on the side table. The glow was feeble. After a couple of seconds, her eyes adapted to the dark and she could see a little bit.

Smudged gray dust outlined a large square on the side table.

She wiped a fingertip across it. Fingerprint dust. It had to be. The peculiar color distinguished it from household dust.

Looking at the table, Christy knew immediately what had lain there. Dad's scrapbook. More pain gnawed at her heart. Ever since she could remember, he'd kept it. How many times had she sat in his lap as he'd pasted pictures of her and baby Autumn in the leather-bound book and carefully, in neat, precise printing, labeled each one with their name, the date and a sweet or funny comment?

But that image quickly morphed into the memory of Detective Ryker Delancey showing her the pages in the back of that beloved book, behind the family pictures. Pages containing baby photos of girls she didn't know, with comments written beside them in a shaky hand she hardly recognized as her father's.

Those were her father's victims, and Detective Ryker Delancey had made her look at them, made her read her father's careful notes about where they lived, when their birthdays were and when he planned to kill them. Then the detective had demanded to know if she'd seen them before.

Of course she'd never seen them. Angrily she swiped her hand across the table's surface, obliterating the dust outline of the book. Did the detective know he'd destroyed every last good memory from her childhood? Did he care?

She dusted her hands together. She should leave. She knew she wasn't supposed to cross crime-scene tape. But this was her home, or it had been. Didn't she have a right?

She glanced desperately around the dimly lit room, hoping to find something—anything—that would give her an explanation for why her father had done what he had. Something rational that she could take to the police and say, "Here, look. This is what he was doing. Now it makes sense, doesn't it?"

But she knew there was nothing to find. No rational explanation, no sane reason.

She blinked and realized her gaze had settled on a framed picture Autumn had drawn of their mother. It hung on the wall above the television. Christy's eyes filled with tears. Their mother had been beautiful and smart. Autumn had looked just like her. She stepped over and touched the glass. More dust. She sneezed.

Guilt and embarrassment tightened her chest, making it difficult to breathe. Anyone coming into this sad house would immediately see how badly she'd neglected her father.

She reached into her purse for a tissue.

"Freeze!" a harsh voice barked.

Shocked, she turned. The unmistakable silhouette of a uniformed police officer darkened the doorway.

"Wait!" she called out, her hand still inside her purse. "I'm—"

"I said freeze!"

She froze.

The harsh beam of a flashlight swept her, blinding her as it passed over her face. Finally, the beam stopped on her hands.

"Hold it!" he barked when she started to pull her hand out of her purse. "Don't move that hand."

"Oh, no. It's okay. I was just—"

"Stop! Now I want you to lift your hand out of your purse, thumb up."

Christy frowned, but tried to comply. She raised her hand until her thumb was visible over the edge of the purse's clasp.

"Okay," the officer said, his gun still pointed at her, his eyes bright in the dimness of the doorway. "Now—slowly, lift your hand all the way out, and if I see *anything* in it, I'll shoot."

Numb with fear, she did what he said, spreading her shaky fingers to demonstrate that they were empty.

The officer's stance relaxed a bit. "Drop your purse. Do it!"

She dropped it.

"How'd you get in here?"

"Please," she said. "I'm—"

"How?"

"My key. It's in my purse."

The officer shone the beam of the flashlight in her face again. "Are you alone?" he asked.

"Yes. Of course."

"Step outside," he continued, backing across the threshold. "Keep your hands where I can see them."

She complied, following him until she was on the porch and he had backed down the steps to the sidewalk. She saw the police car parked behind her rental car.

"Who are you?" he snapped, once he got a look at her in the afternoon sunlight.

"Chr-Christmas Leigh Moser. Albert Moser is my father."

"Your father?" He rubbed a hand across the bald top of his head.

She understood the slight note of bewilderment in his voice. Until twelve days ago she'd thought the same thing. Serial killers didn't have daughters, families, lives.

"Don't you know you're not supposed to cross crime-scene tape?"

Christy shrugged carefully. "I'm sorry," she said innocently. "I've never been involved in a crime before."

The officer touched the microphone on his shoulder. "Sneed here. I'm at the Moser scene. Cancel backup. It's the perp's daughter." He aimed a stern gaze at her. "You need to leave, ma'am. If you go to the sheriff's office over on

Columbia Street and fill out the proper paperwork, you can get access to the scene once the crime lab has released it."

Horror enveloped her like a dark cloud. "The *perp?* The *crime lab?*" Her stomach turned over again and acrid saliva filled her mouth. She swallowed hard.

"Why is my father's house a crime scene?" she demanded, her voice hollow to her own ears. "He didn't do anything here." She shuddered as the scrapbook's pages rose before her inner vision and the court bailiff's bland voice listing the women her father had killed played over in her mind. "Did he?"

He sniffed. "The suspect's residence has been declared part of the crime scene, as have his vehicles."

"I see," she said, feeling numb. "Thank you."

The policeman gestured toward her car. "Now get on out of here," he said as he holstered his gun.

She had no choice but to obey him. She walked past him down the sidewalk. As she did, the microphone attached to his shoulder crackled. The only words she could make out were *Moser* and *hospital.*

"What?" she exclaimed, turning back toward him. Her heart thudded painfully. Her father? Hospital? Oh, no!

The policeman spoke into his mic. "I've got the daughter here. I'll let her know."

"Ms. Moser," he said. "That was the dispatcher. Your father has suffered a heart attack. He's being taken to St. Tammany Parish Medical Center."

"Oh, no!" Christy breathed. "Not again!" She started toward her car.

"Ma'am?" the officer called after her. "I can get you there faster in the squad car."

Christy stopped in her tracks. "Thank you," she said.

As she got into the police car and the officer cranked it and sped away, blue lights flashing, she prayed, "Please don't let my father die before I get there. I need to tell him how sorry I am."

THREE HOURS LATER, after her father had been moved from the emergency room to the cardiac care unit, Christy left the hospital. The nurse in charge had told her that she wouldn't be able to see him again until morning. She argued that she was a physician and demanded to see the doctor in charge. But when the cardiac specialist found out she was a pediatrician, he'd smiled apologetically and told her the same thing. It was a hospital policy. Intensive-care visiting hours must be observed—by everyone.

So she'd called a taxi to take her back to her dad's house to pick up her rental car. Then, exhausted, she headed to the Oak Grove Inn, a bed-and-breakfast she'd booked in Chef Voleur, stopping along the way to pick up a bottle of wine.

After her flight the night before, she'd barely had time to unload her bags and fall into bed. Then this morning she'd been up at dawn, unable to sleep with her father's nine o'clock sentencing hearing looming. Now more than twelve hours later, her dad was in the hospital, and all she wanted to do was go back there and sit with him. But she couldn't. The last thing the nurse had told her was to rest. "It's the best thing you can do for your father now. It won't help him if you're exhausted."

Irritatingly, it was the same thing she told worn-out parents of her young patients. It was bitter medicine to swallow, but she knew the nurse was right.

She took a deep breath and squeezed her burning eyes shut. She vowed to take the nurse's advice.

As she approached the inn, which was on a quiet street in a residential section of Chef Voleur, she thought about the difference between the north shore of the Pontchartrain and Boston. As much as the north shore had grown over the last twenty years, the cities still retained a lot of small-town character.

She pulled into the small parking lot. A loud roar announced a big pickup pulling in beside her. Living in Boston for six years, she'd forgotten how many pickups were on the roads in Louisiana. She couldn't remember ever seeing one in Boston proper.

She got out, grabbed her purse and the bag holding the wine and headed for her cottage, sending a vague smile toward the darkened windows of the pickup. As she walked past the main house toward the third of four tiny cottages lined up behind it, a motion-sensing light came on. But her cottage was dark. Someone—the maid?—had turned off the light she'd deliberately left on this morning.

Behind her, heavy footsteps crunched on the tiny seashells that were mixed with gravel to form the path to the cottages. The driver of the pickup, probably.

Her big-city instincts kicked in and she clutched her purse tightly against her ribs as she quickly inserted the key into the door and turned it.

The crunching footsteps came closer.

It's just the person in Cottage Four, she told herself as she opened the door to slip inside.

A crushing blow hit her on the back and sent her sprawling onto the floor.

Chapter Two

When the blow slammed Christy to the floor, the bag containing the bottle of wine flew out of her hands and landed with a thud in front of her.

Still driven by the momentum of the blow and the weight against her, she pitched forward, hands out to break her fall. She hit the hardwood floor hard and felt a distinct, painful snap in her right wrist.

Pain and panic immobilized her for an instant as a heavy body landed on top of her. He straddled her, pinning her down.

Her heart pounded violently and her limbs quivered. The man grabbed a fistful of her hair and slammed her face down onto the hardwood floor. He put his mouth near her ear. She could smell stale cigarettes on his breath.

She tried to suck in enough air to scream, but his weight pressing her chest into the hardwood floor was too heavy. She tried anyway. All that came from her lips was a feeble squeak.

"Shut your mouth," his gravely voice whispered.

Christy's hands were pinned underneath her, and her right wrist pulsed with a sickening pain. Using her left hand, she tried to move, to roll, anything to get him off her. Nothing worked and every tiny movement intensified the piercing agony in her broken wrist. It was making her nauseous.

Whatever the man intended to do to her, she couldn't stop him. He was too strong and she was too weak.

"Please—" she rasped. "What do you want—?"

His hand pushed her cheek harder into the floor. "Go back where you came from," he growled. "Or you're as dead as your sister."

Terror sliced through her like a razor blade. *Her sister's killer.* He'd followed her. Just as the thoughts whirled through her brain, he grabbed her hair again and banged her head against the floor—twice. The blows stunned her.

At some point, she was aware that his crushing weight was gone. Dazed, her head spinning and her wrist throbbing, she managed to roll over onto her side.

Where was he? Dear God—she couldn't see anything in the dark. Was he really gone? Or was he hiding in the shadows, preparing to kill her?

Instinctively she reached for the tiny can of Mace she carried in her pocket, but when she moved her hand, the pain nearly took her breath away.

She rolled onto her back and tried to reach it with her left hand. It was awkward—almost impossible. Tears welled in her eyes and slid down her cheeks. Tears of frustration, of pain, of paralyzing fear.

Finally, she got her fingers on the object in her pocket, but it wasn't the Mace. It was her smart phone.

Desperately she grabbed it, trying to press the buttons for 911. But her fingers were shaking too badly. The device slipped from her fumbling fingers and clattered across the hardwood floor.

No!

"Help!" she whispered, her lungs deflated by sobbing. She rolled onto her stomach and reached out with her left hand, feeling along the floor. Where was it?

"Where are you?"

She gasped, at first thinking it was her attacker's voice. But no. This voice was tinny, mechanical. Was it her phone? She squinted.

There. She saw the light from the display. Thank God. But it was halfway across the room.

Forcing a deep breath into her spasming lungs, she tried to pull herself up enough to crawl toward it, but her right wrist was useless. Worse than useless. If it didn't stop throbbing, she was going to throw up. The pain was making her sick.

Giving up on trying to move, she cried, "Help me!"

God, what was the name of this place? Her brain was so fuzzy, and she hurt so bad. "Three—! she cried breathlessly. "Cottage Three," Christy sobbed. "Please hurry!"

REILLY DROVE LIKE A bat out of hell toward the Oak Grove Inn. What if he was wrong? What if he'd misunderstood Christy Moser's sobbing words? The only *cottages* he knew about were on Oak Street in Chef Voleur, about two miles from his Covington high-rise condo.

He should have asked her where she was staying when he'd gotten her phone number. Now it was too late. Something had happened to the beautiful black-haired serial killer's daughter, and she'd called him—because his number was the latest number in her phone.

"Christy? Christy can you hear me?" he yelled into his phone. "Hang on. It's Reilly Delancey. I'll be right there." He kept talking to her because the line was still open. He had no idea whether she could hear him or not. Holding his breath, he listened. Was that a sob? Or harsh, panicked breathing?

"Christy. Talk to me. Where is Cottage Three? Is it Oak Grove Inn?"

"Oak—?"

Fear arrowed through him at her weak, rasping voice. "Christy? I'm coming. Hang in there."

He careered around the corner onto Oak Street and into the driveway of the B&B. His brain registered three vehicles in the parking lot. A silver Avalon with rental plates, a light blue pickup with Louisiana plates and a Prius with a Mississippi vanity tag that said LVG CPL. He pulled into the parking lot beside the pickup and vaulted out of his car.

Cottage Three. As he sprinted toward the row of small cottages lined up on the grounds of the Oak Grove Bed-and-Breakfast he grabbed his weapon and flashlight from his belt.

"Hey!" he shouted. "Guerrant! Guerrant, you in there?" The owner, Guerrant Bardin, lived in the back of the main house. "Call the police!"

"What the hell?" he heard just as a motion-sensing light flared.

"Call 911!" Reilly shouted. "Get the police over here. A woman's been attacked."

More lights came on. He saw Bardin standing on his back porch in boxer shorts and a T-shirt, with his phone at his ear.

The door to Cottage Three was standing open. Reilly slowed down and approached carefully, holding his gun and his flashlight ready.

He rounded the door facing and the flashlight's beam hit a female body sprawled on the hardwood floor.

Christy! Horror turned his blood to ice. Then she moved and gasped, and relief flooded him. Automatically, he swept the room with the flashlight's beam and called out to no one in particular, "Clear."

Then he crouched beside the black-haired beauty and brushed her silky hair out of her face. "Christy?" he said softly. "Hey, Christy, talk to me."

"No—" she moaned, trying to push him away.

"It's okay. I'm Reilly Delancey—" He took a breath. "The police," he clarified.

At that instant, crunching footsteps approached. Reilly whirled, aiming flashlight and gun at the doorway. "Hold it right there," he barked.

"What's going on?" a voice growled. He heard the unmistakable sound of a shotgun shell being chambered.

"Guerrant? It's Reilly Delancey. Did you call the police?"

"Hell yeah, I did." Bardin stepped into the doorway and reached around to flip on the lights. He'd pulled on blue jeans over his boxers. "Oh, crap. What happened?"

"I think she was attacked. Don't touch anything. Wait out there for the police."

"Is she alive?"

As Bardin spoke, Christy moved her right arm and cried out in obvious pain.

With the lights on, Reilly saw that her slim skirt was ripped, her stockings were torn and one foot was bare. Beyond her, toward the bathroom, her purse had slid across the floor and spilled. A bottle of wine in a paper bag had rolled into a corner. Her phone lay just out of her reach.

"Guerrant, guard the door. If you see anything, holler. I need to clear the area." Reilly slipped out the door of the cottage and canvassed the area. He didn't see anyone. He checked the seashell-and-gravel path that connected the cottages. It ended at the fence that surrounded the inn's grounds. The fence was green chicken wire, designed to disappear amid the landscaping. It would be absurdly easy for someone to climb it and vault over. He shone the flashlight into the thicket on the other side of the fence. Nothing.

He circled around the cottages, just to be sure there was nobody lurking, then walked up to the door where Guerrant was standing guard.

"Didn't see anybody here," Guerrant reported.

When Reilly entered, Christy was struggling to sit up. She looked up at him. There was a scrape on her cheek. She blinked. "Reilly Delancey," she said hoarsely. "Not the detective."

"Are you okay? Are you hurt?"

She squeezed her eyes shut. "The scaphoid bone in my wrist is fractured, although it's not displaced. Please help me up."

Scaphoid bone? Reilly had no idea what she'd just told him, but he had heard the words *wrist* and *fractured*. "No. You stay right there. Don't move. I'm calling—"

Christy pushed herself up using her left hand and pressed her right hand protectively against her ribs.

"—the EMTs," Reilly finished with a sigh. Super-confident. Super-cool, even after being attacked. Even with a broken wrist. Did that come from being a physician? Or from what must have been a very difficult childhood? Either way, he was glad she was alive.

Giving up on the notion that she might listen to him, he crouched beside her, ready to steady her if she felt faint or got sick. She looked a little green around the gills.

"Help me up," she ordered. When she tried to move, her mouth tightened and the tension along her jawline increased.

He had his phone out. "No. You'll wait for the ambulance—" he started.

Using just her left arm, she struggled to get her feet under her. With a sigh, he slid his hands under her arms and helped her to her feet. "Do you ever listen?"

"I—know my own body," she replied, putting a notion in Reilly's head that he quickly banished.

She teetered between one high heel and one bare foot. Earlier at the courthouse, he'd observed that she was just about as tall as his nearly six feet. But now, as she put her weight on her bare foot, she seemed small. Her shoulders under his hand felt bony—feminine—sexy.

She still appeared dazed, and if the situation weren't so dire, she might have looked comically awkward with one shoe on and one shoe off. He gently pushed her down into the chair, a little surprised when she didn't protest.

He watched her carefully. She held her wrist cradled against her, protecting it. A large red area on her forehead was swelling and turning purple. Her lips were white at the corners. The scrape on her left cheek blossomed with tiny beads of blood, like early morning dew on a red flower.

She caught him checking out the scrape. "It's nothing more than an abrasion." She tentatively pressed it with a finger. "I'll probably have a mild contusion," she said, then added, "a bruise." She frowned. "And a larger one on my forehead."

"Your wrist—" Reilly started.

"I told you, it's not displaced. It won't need setting. I'll wrap it and get a wrist guard. There's no need for medical treatment."

"That's not your call," Reilly informed her as he dialed one-handed. "What happened?"

She shook her head as if trying to clear it and touched the bruise on her forehead. "I was hit from behind. Knocked to the floor. I thought—" She stopped.

Reilly ordered an ambulance then hung up. "You thought what?"

She shook her head again. "Nothing. The man said, 'Go back where you came from or you're as dead as your sister.'"

The words shocked Reilly. "He said that? Those exact words? Are you sure?"

"Yes."

Although she looked like a frightened, hurt young woman, her reply was confident and smooth.

"What else did he say?"

"Nothing. He got off me and left."

"Did you get a good look at him?"

She shook her head. "I tried to turn over and get up but my wrist—" Her voice gave out.

"You're positive it was a man?" Reilly asked.

She looked at him frowning. "Of course."

"Why 'of course'?"

But before she could answer, the crunch of heavy boots on seashells and gravel announced the arrival of the police. Two uniformed officers appeared at the door to the cottage, their weapons drawn.

Reilly indicated the badge at his belt. "Deputy Reilly Delancey, SWAT. Dr. Moser here was attacked." He didn't know the officers, but both of them glanced his way when he told them his name. He'd long since stopped being surprised by that.

In and around Chef Voleur the name Delancey always drew a reaction. Depending on the situation and the people, the reactions were vastly different. Reilly figured the two officers knew or had heard of Ryker.

One of the officers stepped over to Christy and the other faced him.

"Delancey? Deputy Buford Watts. How'd you get here?"

"Dr. Moser is involved with a case of my brother's, Detective Ryker Delancey. I had given her my phone number in case she couldn't reach him."

The officer's gaze sharpened. "Moser. Not—the October Killer?"

"There's no reason to get into that," Reilly responded, knowing as soon as the words left his mouth that he was wrong. Given what her attacker had said, there was definitely a reason to get into that.

"No? Do you know who attacked her?"

"Not yet."

"Her father killed half-a-dozen women," Watts said, his gaze studying her.

Four, Reilly corrected silently, sending an apologetic look toward Christy. The deputy was being deliberately insensitive.

"What if it was a victim's family member?" Watts continued. "Have you gotten specifics?"

"Just got here myself," Reilly answered. "I'd like to be in on your interview though."

The officer didn't have any objection. Within a few minutes, Christy, who was still refusing medical treatment, Reilly and the two officers were seated at the dining room table in the main house of Oak Grove Inn.

"Now, Ms. Moser," the first officer started.

"It's *Doctor* Moser," Reilly inserted, just as Bardin's wife bustled in, wrapped in a voluminous fleece robe.

"For goodness sakes! What are you doing to this poor girl?"

Reilly tensed at Ella Bardin's use of the word *girl*. He glanced at Christy sidelong, trying to send her a signal not to insult Ella, but she wasn't paying any attention to Ella's choice of words or to him. She was staring into space and frowning.

"Get out of the way, all of you," Ella continued.

"Ella—" said the older officer.

"Buford Watts, you just hold your horses." Ella turned to Christy. "I've put some water on to boil, and I'll get you a cup of tea in just a minute, unless you'd rather have coffee?"

Christy realized that Ella was talking to her. She looked

up and her stiff demeanor softened just a little, barely enough to notice. "Oh, thank you. Tea is fine."

"And here." Ella Bardin stepped over to a recliner and pulled an afghan off the back of it. "Cover up with this. The very idea—" this aimed at the three men "—of leaving her sitting there in that torn skirt. What kind of gentlemen are you?"

Watts answered, "The kind who're trying to find out who attacked her, Miss Ella." His words were measured.

The younger officer grinned at Ella. "I sure could use something warm to drink, Miss Ella."

Ella looked at him. "I'm sure you could," she retorted as she started back toward the kitchen.

Watts turned his attention back to Christy. "Dr. Moser, could you tell me your full name please?"

She straightened. "Christmas Leigh Moser. That's L-E-I-G-H."

Watts's eyebrows raised, then lowered.

Reilly's did too. *Christmas.* He thought about what Christy had said about her sister, and remembered Ryker mentioning Moser's other daughter. Her name was odd too. Summer? No, Autumn.

He assessed Dr. Christmas Leigh Moser. Somehow, the name, which could easily have seemed silly, fit her. He wasn't sure why he thought that.

Buford Watts wrote something on his pad, then addressed Christy again. "Good. Now if you would, tell me exactly what happened."

"Certainly," she said coolly. "As you obviously already know, my father is Albert Moser." She waited for confirmation from the officers. They nodded.

"I flew in from Boston late last night." She paused. "I had to find physicians to take my patients before I could leave," she explained. "I went to his arraignment this morning. Then this afternoon I received a call that he had suffered an MI—a heart attack, so I went to the hospital." She stopped to take a fortifying breath. "He's in the cardiac care unit. I left there around six o'clock, stopped at a liquor store to pick up a bottle of wine, then drove here, to the inn. I parked in the lot out there."

"That's your car? The rental?" Deputy Watts asked.

She nodded. "Just as I parked the car, a light-colored pickup pulled in next to me. I walked to my cottage—Cottage Three," she amended. "I unlocked the door, but before I could enter, something hit me from behind. The blow knocked me to the floor. I landed on my wrist and fractured the scaphoid bone."

Both officers' gazes went to her right hand, which she held against her torso. At that moment, Reilly saw the flash of red lights through Ella Bardin's lace curtains and heard the crunch of tires on shells and gravel. "There's the ambulance," he said, earning him an angry glance from Christy.

"I told you—" she started, but he sent her a look that his brother Ryker had dubbed "The Silencer." It worked. She pressed her lips together and merely glared at him.

The EMTs made quick work of her broken wrist. For the most part, she'd been right. There was little that could be done about the bone that was broken. The EMTs iced it for a few minutes, then applied a pink cast that covered her palm and half of her thumb, and extended about four inches up her forearm.

"You need to ice your forehead too," he said, scrutinizing the bruised skin. "It'll help keep the swelling down, and maybe prevent a black eye."

"I know," she responded archly.

The EMT glanced over at Reilly, then applied a small bandage to her cheek. The bandage was also pink, with ladybugs on it.

Reilly was pretty sure Christy had no idea what was on the bandage. The wink one of the EMTs gave him on the way out confirmed it. Their way of getting her back for lecturing them about the futility of putting a cast on a scaphoid fracture.

Once the EMTs were gone, the officers resumed the questioning.

"You were saying that someone knocked you to the floor," Buford Watts prompted her.

She adjusted the ice pack. "Yes. I'd just unlocked and opened the door when I was hit from behind. The man landed on top of me. I tried to roll over, or buck or kick, but he was too heavy."

Reilly noticed a faint shiver tense her muscles. He doubted the officers saw it. They seemed mesmerized by her striking appearance, or maybe her calm recitation of what had happened.

Watts asked the question Reilly had asked her before. "You know it was a man? Did you get a good look at him?"

"No." A sharp syllable. "I was on my stomach and he was on top of me. But it was a man. No question." She met each officer's gaze, but didn't look at Reilly. Then she took a deep breath. "I know because he was straddling me."

Reilly's breath stuck in his throat. "Did he—?" he croaked, earning a stiff glance from the officer in charge. This wasn't Reilly's case. Not technically. For their purposes, he was merely a witness—the first person the victim had called.

Christy Moser looked directly at him for the first time since they'd come into the house. As before, when he'd looked into her eyes at the coffee kiosk, he thought he saw something underneath their cool darkness.

She gave a slight negative shake of her head. "I wasn't raped," she said quickly. "But it was obvious that he was male."

The younger officer's face turned pink. "Yes, ma'am,"

he said, then cleared his throat. "Did he—did he take anything?"

She shook her head. "Nothing. Apparently his only purpose in attacking me was to give me a message."

"A message?" the officer echoed.

Christy opened her mouth but before she could speak, Ella Bardin was back with a steaming mug of fragrant tea. "Here you go, dear. I'm sorry it took so long, but I wanted to wait until the EMTs were gone."

The two officers eyed the hot drink with covetousness in their gazes, but if Ella Bardin noticed, she gave no sign of it. Christy thanked her and held the cup in her left hand.

"You said the attacker left you a *message?*"

"That's right. He pushed my face against the hardwood floor and said, 'Go back where you came from or you're as dead as your sister.'"

Reilly watched the two officers. Both of them sat up straight in their seats.

"Your sister?" Watts said.

At the same time the younger officer echoed, "Get out of town?"

Christy Moser held up the hand with the cast. Her fingernails were perfectly manicured, except for the right index one, which was raggedly broken. "Let me explain," she said, much more calmly than the officers' outbursts. She took a quick breath and continued.

"My sister was murdered five years ago, on Bienville Street in the French Quarter. Her death was ruled a mugging, but my father was certain that she was murdered by a married man with whom she was having an affair. The night she died was her birthday and she'd gone down to the Quarter to celebrate."

The word *celebrate* took on an ironic tone. Reilly wondered just how much Christy knew about her sister and the man she'd been seeing.

"I've been in Boston for the past six years, doing a residency and then a fellowship in pediatrics at Children's Hospital. I had—" She paused and a fleeting shadow crossed her face. "I wasn't aware of everything that was going on. However, I believe that my attack this evening proves that my father was right. My sister's death wasn't just a mugging. And apparently whoever killed her feels threatened by my presence here."

Reilly noticed that the two officers seemed bewildered. He sympathized with them. He'd barely kept up with her rapid-fire explanation and conclusion, and he had the advantage of knowing something about the case from Ryker.

The lead officer looked at Reilly then back at Christy. "I think we need to get an official statement from you— downtown. And I'm going to call CSI to look for trace from the man who allegedly assaulted you."

"Allegedly?" Her voice was frosty.

"Legal terminology," Reilly commented in an effort to soften the officer's words. He was afraid if Christy stiffened any more, she'd break.

Turning to Watts, he said, "Can the statement wait until tomorrow? Dr. Moser is exhausted."

Watts sent him a glaring look, but nodded. "Sure. We can take the official statement tomorrow. But Ms.—Dr. Moser, you might want to give some thought to what you want in the official record. If you're prepared to make a written sworn statement to everything you've just told us, then you are accusing the man who assaulted you and threatened your life of killing your sister. If we're able to find any trace evidence and match it to someone, your statement accuses that person of murder."

Christy waited a few seconds, watching the officer closely,

but he didn't say anything else. She nodded. "That's exactly right, Officer. I am definitely accusing the man who attacked me of murdering my sister."

Chapter Three

After the police finished questioning Christy, they cordoned off and locked Cottage Three, holding it as a crime scene until the CSI team could process it the next day.

Ella Bardin insisted that Christy sleep in the front bedroom of the main house of the Oak Grove Inn, the Lakeview Room. It didn't look out over any lake Reilly had ever seen, but there were photos of famous lakes all over the room, including Lake Pontchartrain. After Ella made sure the room was in perfect condition, she excused herself, saying she had an early morning. Tomorrow was French toast day and she had to get up at five o'clock.

Reilly deposited the few items the officers had allowed Christy to grab from her cottage onto the antique dresser and turned to say good-night to her.

She was standing in the middle of the room, watching him carefully. She definitely looked the worse for wear. She'd twisted her glossy black hair into some kind of knot, but it was coming undone. Her torn skirt would have been indecent if not for the black lace slip. Her stockings were in shreds, and she'd long since discarded the single shoe and her jacket.

Her expression reflected her experience. It was at once angry, bewildered, frustrated and scared. Reilly felt an odd urge to cross the room and pull her into his arms. But Dr.

Christmas Moser wouldn't appreciate him peeking beneath her tough exterior. In fact, he knew what she'd say if he tried to offer comfort.

That does not accomplish anything, Officer. Surely you realize that.

"I heard your father had a heart attack," he said. "He's in the cardiac unit?"

She nodded.

"I'm sorry. You don't need any more stress right now."

"What's on your mind, Officer Delancey?"

The question surprised him. He'd already noticed her keen observation of the officers as they checked out her and her story. His grandmother's saying, "doesn't miss a trick," certainly applied to her.

"I'm not sure what you mean," he parried.

"I doubt that."

He inclined his head in agreement. If she was up to answering questions he had plenty to ask. "All right. How long did you say you'd been in Boston?"

"Six years." She reached up with her right hand to push a strand of hair out of her eyes and winced when the cast got in her way.

"Six years. And did you say you hadn't been home?"

"No. That's not what I said," she answered firmly, although Reilly thought he saw a flicker in her eyes that indicated that she wasn't telling the whole truth. As a sniper and sometimes leader of the hostage negotiation team for the St. Tammany Parish SWAT team, he'd made it a practice to study kinesiology—facial expressions, body language, all indicators of stress.

"I believe I said I hadn't known how badly my father was taking Autumn's death. Of course I've been home in the past six years."

"How many times?"

Christy lifted her chin. "Is all this on the record, Officer?"

He shook his head.

"Then I'd rather wait and give my statement once only, at the police station."

"No problem," he said. "I'll pick you up at eight o'clock, out front."

Her eyes went wide. "What?"

He smiled and nodded toward her right hand. "You can't very well drive with that cast on."

"Certainly I can," she shot back, but her right fingers twitched.

"Yeah? Touch each of your fingers to your thumb."

She set her mouth and lifted her hand. But the cast was too restrictive. She couldn't make her fingers and thumb touch. "I told the EMTs not to immobilize my thumb," she complained.

"Eight o'clock," he repeated. He thought he heard a feminine growl. "And in the meantime, you call me if you need me."

"There's no reason for you to appoint yourself my chauffeur. I'll take a taxi."

Reilly lay his hand on the cast where it covered her knuckles. "There is a reason. You asked me to help you."

She looked at his hand, then up at him. One day, he promised himself, he was going to explore that vulnerability she kept locked behind her snapping green eyes.

"I thought you were your brother at the time."

"Still," Reilly said with a grin. "You did ask. And you called me when you were attacked. I figure that makes it my responsibility to keep you safe. I have no intention of letting that guy get within a hundred yards of you. Consider me your knight in shining armor, until I'm sure you're no longer in danger."

"I don't need a knight—"

"Don't start with me, damsel," he said teasingly, touching her lips with his forefinger. "Whether you think you need me or not, you've got me."

CHRISTY WAS FUMING by the time Reilly Delancey left. She prided herself on being able to handle any situation. As a pediatrician specializing in trauma, her working life was all about emergencies.

Involving kids. Not herself. She glared at the cast on her wrist. How careless of her to break her wrist. Still, it shouldn't hinder her too much. As if to mock her, a throbbing ache began beneath the cast.

Reilly Delancey was a bully. Somehow, and she wasn't sure how, he'd gotten her to agree to ride with him. She sniffed. It was ridiculous. She could drive. A simple wrist cast wouldn't be that big a problem.

She wriggled the fingers of her right hand. A shooting pain made her gasp. Well, she amended, she could drive if she had to.

She was disgusted with herself. She should have been more careful. She'd seen dozens of children with wrist fractures because they instinctively reached out to break their fall. Tucking arms into the body and rolling was much safer. *If* one had time to react.

To be fair, she'd had no time. But now she had to live with a pink cast for several weeks.

She held up her hand and grimaced. *Pink*. Her colleagues in Boston would give her hell about that. Almost any color would have been better than pink. But the EMT had sworn the only colors of paste he had were pink or fluorescent green.

Now that she thought about it, wasn't the color added after

the paste was mixed? And wasn't the default color of the paste white? At the time she hadn't felt like protesting. So she had a pink cast and there was nothing she could do about it tonight.

She glanced at her watch. After ten o'clock. Reilly Delancey had told her he'd pick her up at eight in the morning. She needed to get some sleep.

Stepping into the bathroom, she reached up with her left hand to loosen her hair as she looked in the mirror. And stopped cold.

The EMT had applied a pink strip bandage with ladybugs on it. *Ladybugs.* She frowned at her image. Reilly Delancey was behind this. She was sure of it. He was nothing but trouble, and she didn't need any more trouble than she already had.

She quickly undressed, dropping the skirt and the shredded stockings into the trash can in the bathroom. Digging into her suitcase, she unearthed her pink satin pajamas.

Staring at them, her face flamed, even though she was alone. Damn those EMTs and Reilly Delancey. How had he known—?

She stopped that thought right there. He couldn't have known that she loved wearing pretty, feminine lingerie under her utilitarian work clothes. Although—his blue eyes *were* awfully sharp, and it looked as if he never missed a trick.

After a painful few minutes spent getting the pajamas on, she turned back the covers awkwardly and climbed into bed. But when she tried to relax and clear her mind, she couldn't stop her thoughts from racing.

—where you came from or you're as dead as your sister.

—Mr. Moser, do you understand that by pleading guilty, you are giving up your right to a trial?

—I did it. I killed those girls.

Your father has had a heart attack—

Christy turned over and squeezed her eyes shut. But closed eyes couldn't block the mental image of the emergency room technician loading all the heart monitors and IVs onto her father's gurney and wheeling him onto the elevator to take him up to the cardiac care unit.

Christy hadn't been able to take her eyes off her dad. Against the white sheets he looked small, frail, vulnerable. He looked nothing like the man who'd reared her and her sister.

Her eyes stung and hot tears squeezed out between her closed lids. Sniffling and telling herself that tears never solved a problem, she turned over again and tried to find a comfortable position for her wrist.

But despite her resolve, the tears kept on coming. They slid over the bridge of her nose and down her cheek to the pillow. When had her family fallen apart? When had her dad changed from a big, strong parent, raising two daughters on his own, into a deranged killer?

WHEN REILLY GOT TO THE Oak Grove Inn the next morning, Christy was waiting in the foyer.

"Morning," he said with a smile, which faded as he took in her injuries. "Wow, they weren't kidding about that bruise. Did you put ice on your forehead?"

"Of course. Otherwise I *would* have a black eye. You're late."

Reilly nodded. "Miss Ella caught me as I was leaving last night. She told me to wait until eight-thirty so you could eat breakfast. French toast day today, right?" He reached out and wiped a speck of powdered sugar off her chin. "Hard to eat with a cast on, isn't it? Think how tough it would be to drive."

Christy swiped at her chin with two fingers. "Are you ready to go?"

"Yep." He opened the front door and stepped aside to let her precede him out the door. This morning she had on brown pants and a cream-colored top with long sleeves that stretched over the cast on her wrist and a short brown sweater. He didn't see any buttons anywhere. She'd picked an outfit that was easy to don.

"You look nice," he commented as he followed her to his car.

"Thank you," she said stiffly. She reached for the passenger-door handle with her left hand, but he stretched around her and opened the door. When he did, her hair brushed his cheek. A bolt of lightning-hot lust shot straight to his groin.

Damn. His reaction surprised him. So much that he'd almost gasped. He immediately straightened, putting the door between him and her, but not before his nose caught a subtle floral scent that was very familiar to him. Christy Moser smelled like the gardenias that grew in his grandmother Lilibelle's garden.

As Christy climbed into the car, Reilly swallowed. When had he gone from merely admiring her figure and feeling protective of her to lusting after her? Of course, as soon as he asked the question he knew the answer. About two seconds after he'd first spotted her walking across the courthouse lobby.

In fact, he'd woken up in a very uncomfortable state this morning, with the dregs of a sexy dream involving the two of them and dozens of ladybugs floating in his head.

He tried to make small talk on the way to the sheriff's office. He pointed out the Christmas decorations that lined the streets of Covington and made comments about Christmas in the South, where shorts and sandals were more appropriate attire than parkas and boots.

Christy seemed distracted, staring out the window at nothing. Probably thinking about her attack the night before and the statement she was going to have to make in a few minutes.

As he pulled into the parking lot at the sheriff's office, she turned to him. "I never heard from Detective Delancey. I need to talk to him."

Reilly winced. He'd forgotten to call Ryker. "I'll let him know. I'm going to see him this morning." He wanted to ask Ryker about Autumn Moser's case. Whether, after Albert Moser's confession and the connection between the murders he committed and his daughter's death, the case was going to be reopened.

If it was—

"You told me you'd let him know yesterday."

"Yes, I did," he said rather testily. "But the day got busy, for you as well as me." He cut the engine and got out of the car. He knew that Christy had more than one reason to be upset and irritable. And he couldn't deny how beautiful and sexy she was, but he was getting a little tired of her officious attitude.

He walked around the car and opened the passenger door for her.

"Thank you," she muttered as she got out. He followed her into the building and directed her down the hall to the interview rooms.

Buford Watts was standing near the break room, drinking a cup of coffee. When he saw them, he set the coffee mug down on the top of a bookcase and stepped up to Christy.

"Morning, Ms. Moser."

Reilly started to correct him, then bit his tongue. If Christy wanted to remind the man that she was a doctor, she could do it herself.

"Good morning," she responded evenly.

"I've got a room set up for us. It's right through there." Buford pointed the way to Interview Room Two. The door was open. Christy entered and Reilly followed, but Buford stopped him at the door.

"Don't you have something to do this morning, Delancey?"

Reilly shook his head. "This week the SWAT team is practicing and recertifying weapons skills. I finished yesterday." He gave Buford a bright smile. "You said I could sit in on the interview."

"The interview last night. Nobody said anything about this morning," Buford said.

"Well, do you have a problem with me sitting in?"

The deputy muttered something under his breath and went into the room. Reilly entered behind him. Buford indicated a chair for Christy to sit in, then sat directly across from her, with the tape recorder in the middle of the table.

Reilly moved a chair to a neutral spot at the end of the table, neither on Christy's side nor Buford's.

Buford turned on the tape recorder and went through the required preliminary information—date, name, location and so on. He quickly and casually ran through the questions he'd asked Christy the night before.

Then he leaned forward and picked up a folder that was lying near his right hand. "Ms. Moser—Dr. Moser that is—our crime scene investigator team went over to the Oak Grove Inn this morning and checked out Cottage Three. They didn't find any trace evidence specific to your case."

Christy stiffened. "What do you mean? Are you saying I made up the attack?"

"Now, now, Miss. I'm not doubting you were attacked. That was obvious. But as good a housekeeper as Miss Ella is, there was a lot of hair and dust and stuff on the floor of that cottage. CSI told me they didn't find anything that could be definitely linked to last night."

Christy tried to fold her hands in front of her but the cast interfered. The fingers and thumb of her left hand played with the edge of the cast. Her gaze flickered to Reilly and away.

"What about the pickup that followed me into the parking lot?"

"Well," Buford reached into his pocket for a small notepad. "That belongs to a Chester Ragsdale. He lives over in Covington. Him and his wife had a spat over the weekend, so he's been staying there in Cottage One the past few days. He said he's gonna try to go home today." Buford took a breath. "My partner talked to him and to the couple from Mississippi who were in Cottage Two. None of them saw or heard anything."

Reilly saw and felt Christy's frustration.

"So you're telling me there's nothing you can do to find the man who attacked me?"

"I'd like you to think back on last night. I know you're awfully upset about your daddy. I don't suppose anyone can blame you for that. And I'm sorry to hear that he's in the hospital. But I do have to ask these questions. When the person knocked you down, tell me again what he said."

She eyed him narrowly. "He said, 'Go back where you came from or you're as dead as your sister.'"

Buford tapped his pencil on the desktop and watched it. "And you're sure about that?"

"Yes." The word was coated in frost.

"Why do you think somebody would go to all that trouble to warn you to get out of town?"

"Officer Watts," Christy said in measured tones. "Five years ago, my sister was shot while I was on the phone with her. I heard her scream. I heard the—shots." She took a breath and sent a quick glance toward Reilly. "The only times I've been back in Chef Voleur since her funeral were once for a seminar three years ago, and then two weeks ago. I flew down here to check on my father after I was notified about his first MI, while he was in jail."

"MI?"

"Myocardial infarction—heart attack."

Watts nodded.

Christy brushed her hair back, a typical sign of discomfort or deceit. Reilly didn't think she was being deceitful.

"I flew back to Boston the same day." She stopped and looked at Watts.

He looked at the eraser tip on his pencil, then back up at her. He raised his eyebrows. "You flew in when your father was put in the hospital. What about when he was arrested?"

She shook her head. "I was busy—on call. I couldn't leave my patients."

The detective nodded and wrote something on his note-pad.

"Don't you see?" she asked. "The man who attacked me is the man who killed my sister—" Christy's voice gave out. She swallowed and spread her hands. "He knew I'd be here for the sentencing."

Her words hung in the air. She looked at Buford, then at Reilly, then back at Buford. Her eyes were bright with unshed tears. "Isn't it obvious? The man who killed my sister knows she was on the phone with me. He obviously is worried that I heard something and can identify him."

Reilly didn't say a word. Buford sat still, his eyes on Christy, as if he were weighing her words. Then he sat up straight. "All right. I think that's all for now, Ms. Moser." He reached for the tape recorder.

"What?" Christy stared at him. "That's *all*? Are you saying you don't believe me?"

Buford punched the off button on the recorder, ejected the tape and stuck it into his shirt pocket. Then he pushed his chair back. Its legs screeched along the floor. He stood with a grunt.

"Why, no, ma'am. I'm not saying that at all. I *am* at a loss to explain how this man who you think killed your sister found you, watched you and followed you, when you'd only been in town for around twenty-four hours."

Christy didn't stand. "You're at a *loss?* I don't see how it could be any clearer, Officer. My father's arrest and arraignment were in all the papers. If my father is right about my sister's death, and I believe he is, then the man who killed her is the married man she was seeing." She stopped long enough to take a breath.

"He knew she had a sister. Even if he didn't know who she was talking to on the phone, her phone is missing. Isn't it logical to infer that he took her phone and saw my number? Naturally, he would expect me to show up at the courthouse. It would be simple for him to spot me there and follow me. Wouldn't it?" She addressed that question to Reilly before turning her icy gaze back to Buford Watts.

"I have to agree, Buford," Reilly said. "It's a theory."

Buford nodded his head. "It coulda happened that way. I just can't make a case for it."

Reilly thought of something. "What about her clothes?" he asked.

Buford had picked up his pencil and was studying the end of it. He frowned at Reilly.

"Her clothes. The skirt, jacket and blouse. Did CSI test her clothes?" Reilly asked him.

The older officer picked up the manila folder and paged through the sheets. "I don't reckon they did."

"Nobody thought about testing her clothes?"

Buford sent Reilly a narrow gaze. "You were there, and being so all-fired helpful. Why didn't you think of it? Hell, you coulda hired somebody to do it for you."

Reilly didn't bother answering him. The resentment had been bound to surface sooner or later. He and Ryker both caught a lot of flak because of their infamous, wealthy grandparents. It was no secret that the Delancey grandkids weren't hurting for money, or that a lot of that money had been made in Louisiana politics, off the backs of citizens.

"I put the skirt and stockings in the trash," Christy interjected. "In the bathroom."

"Buford, call them now. Before Ella Bardin puts out the trash. Get the skirt and stockings. Her blouse and jacket too."

Buford nodded irritably and left the room.

Reilly looked at Christy and gave her a rueful shrug.

She sniffed. "Why do you think I left Louisiana?" she said archly.

"It's not the place," he said. "It's the people. There are good people and bad people everywhere."

When she winced, he realized that his words had hit too close to home.

IT WAS AFTER ONE O'CLOCK before Deputy Watts was done with questioning Christy and forcing her to read her transcribed statements. She'd slowly and meticulously made changes to the transcription using her left hand.

To his credit, the deputy had ordered in po' boy sandwiches and iced tea for lunch. To his discredit, the po' boys weren't seafood. They were piled high with ham and cheese and mustard—loads of mustard. Christy had picked at hers, tearing off bits of the delicious French bread and washing it down with sweet tea.

Reilly stayed with her the whole time. She didn't want him to know how much that meant to her. She didn't want anyone to know that. It bothered her that in two days Reilly Delancey had become the one constant in her suddenly out-of-control life.

She'd heard of the Delanceys. Everyone who'd grown up in Louisiana had. Because of their infamous grandfather, they were all stinking rich. Didn't have to work a day if they didn't want to. So why had Reilly and his brother become cops? She assessed Reilly. He looked sincere and genuinely delighted with his sandwich. But she didn't know him. She couldn't take the risk of depending on him.

She'd never allowed herself to depend on anyone—never looked to a man for validation—except her father. She wasn't happy that Reilly Delancey had appointed himself her protector. Even if she had no idea how she'd have gotten through last night and this morning without him.

"Are you sure you don't want something else to eat?" he asked for the third time as he drove her to the hospital to see her father.

"I'm positive," she responded shortly. Her stomach was growling, but she was about to see her father for the first time since he'd been admitted to the cardiac care unit. Even if she could have eaten, she was pretty sure she wouldn't have been able to hold it down.

Reilly placed his hand at the small of her back as they walked through the halls to the doors of the CCU.

"Thanks for bringing me here," she said dismissively. "What time will you pick me up?"

Reilly looked at his watch, then at a sign beside the door. It listed visiting hours as twenty minutes every hour between 7:00 a.m. and 7:00 p.m.

"I've got a few things to do. What if I pick you up at four-thirty? Then you can have three visits with him."

She nodded. "That'll be good. The nurse told me yesterday

that if it wasn't too busy this afternoon, I could stay a little longer." She took a shaky breath and sighed.

"Christy? You're sure you're okay? I can get back here earlier if you need me to."

She shook her head. "No. I need to be with my dad as much as I can, before—"

Reilly gave her a searching look before nodding. "I'll see you at four-thirty then." He turned and headed back toward the front of the building.

She knew what Reilly was thinking, as clearly as if he'd spoken aloud. How could she sit there at her father's bedside, knowing he'd killed four young women? How could she still view him as her dad, as the man who'd reared her and taught her the values she now embraced?

"I don't know," she whispered as she pressed the automatic door opener and showed the nurse her visitor's badge. She braced herself for the woman's reaction when she said, "I'm here to see Albert Moser. I'm his daughter."

Chapter Four

While Christy visited with her father, Reilly searched out Ryker in his office.

"Hey, old man," he greeted his older-by-seven-minutes brother. "How's Nicole?"

His brother's normally solemn face lit up at the mention of his fiancée. "She's fine. The burns on her hands are almost healed."

"Thank God they were only first-degree."

"Thank God I got there before Moser shot her," Ryker said hoarsely.

Reilly had never seen him so passionate about anything or anyone. Things had always come easy for his brother. Ryker had excelled at everything. And beaten Reilly. In high school, Ryker was quarterback, leaving Reilly to settle for wide receiver. Ryker had graduated top of his class. Reilly was second.

Both had joined the St. Tammany Parish Sheriff's Department, but Ryker had gotten the coveted detective position. Reilly, who was the better shot, had been chosen for SWAT.

And now, Ryker was getting married and once again Reilly was one step behind. *One step,* hell—he corrected himself. He wasn't even dating anyone.

"Speaking of Moser," he responded. "I've got a few questions about his daughter's case."

Ryker sent him an arch look. "Moser's daughter that was murdered? That's an NOPD case. It was shelved as a mugging five years ago."

Reilly sat down in the chair across from Ryker's desk. "Albert Moser's older daughter sought me out at the courthouse yesterday. Thought I was you. She gave me an earful before I could get a word in to tell her she had the wrong twin."

"Oh, yeah, *Doctor* Moser. The Ice Queen."

Reilly smiled and shook his head. "Ice Queen? Yeah, not so much. She was attacked last night at her cottage at the Oak Grove Inn."

Ryker sat and pushed folders out of his way. He leaned back. "I heard about the attack. I've just started looking into Autumn's case again to get a better read on Christy's situation. She okay?"

"Broken wrist and contusions."

"How're you involved? Other than your obvious preference for tall gorgeous brunettes. Tell me she doesn't have green eyes."

Reilly pointedly ignored him. "Yesterday, I told her I'd have you get in touch with her, and I gave her my cell number."

"Your cell number. Why didn't you give her mine?" Ryker's blue eyes sparked with mischief.

Reilly didn't bother to answer. "When she was attacked, she managed to grab her phone and quick-dial my number."

"So you were first on scene?"

"Yeah. I called for backup, but by the time I got there the guy was gone." Reilly took a breath. "You won't believe what he said to her."

Ryker waited.

"He told her, 'Get out of town or you're as dead as your sister.'"

"He said that?"

Reilly nodded. "So what did you find out about the case? Is NOPD going to look at it again?"

"Doubt it. I called Dixon Lloyd at the Eighth, down on Royal Street in the Quarter, and got the name of the detective who caught Autumn Moser's case. His name was—" Ryker grabbed a small notepad that lay on the corner of his desk and paged through it for a few seconds. "Fred Samhurst."

Reilly grabbed a piece of paper from Ryker's trash can and made a note. "Samhurst. What'd he have to say?"

"Where are you going with this, kid?"

"Christy could have been killed last night. Her life was threatened. And if the man who attacked her didn't kill her sister, he knows who did."

"Well, Moser never gave up the notion that his daughter was killed by someone she knew. He thought it was a married man. He said his daughter told him the man was obsessive about keeping the affair quiet. Said his reputation and his career would be in jeopardy. Who's handling Christy's case?"

"Wait a minute," Reilly said. "Go back to the married man. His reputation and career would be in jeopardy?"

Ryker shrugged. "That's what he told me. I thought maybe it was someone Moser knew, and that's why she wouldn't tell him. But Moser insisted he didn't know anybody who would be fired if he was caught having an affair."

"But she thought Moser would recognize him?"

"I thought about that. Maybe he wouldn't have *known* the man. Not personally. Maybe the guy was a celebrity or a politician. Someone in the public eye." Ryker leaned back in his chair. "Moser nixed the celebrity idea. Said if the man were rich, Autumn would have made him buy her stuff. He was right about that. There was no sign in her belongings that someone was spending money on her."

"So maybe what he bought her was drugs," Reilly said.

Ryker's brows drew down into a frown. "Why all the questions? What are you up to, kid?"

"I want to help Christy. I want to find the bastard who attacked her and see what he knows. What I don't understand is why no one listened to her father. Why wasn't Autumn Moser's case reopened a long time ago?"

"I can't answer that. I can tell you that the detective who caught the case probably missed something."

Reilly laughed without humor. "Yeah? You think so?"

"Do you want to hear what I know? I've got plenty to do. I could just let you dig it up yourself."

"Don't go all big-brother master detective on me, Ryker." Reilly hated it when Ryker took that supercilious attitude.

"Fine. Dixon didn't want to rag on a fellow detective, but he did tell me that a couple of years ago Samhurst had a mild heart attack. Said he lost a lot of weight—maybe thirty pounds or so—which left him about forty pounds overweight."

"Are you kidding me? He was that overweight and out of shape? No telling what he missed. How in hell is he still on active duty?"

Ryker shrugged. "Everybody's shorthanded."

"What else did Dixon tell you?"

"Nothing. I talked to Samhurst, but he didn't have much to say. He got real defensive and claimed he didn't remember much. I asked him why three point-blank shots to the chest didn't throw up a red flag, but he didn't have an answer."

"Three shots to the chest? That's how she died? Holy—" Reilly felt a sick weight in his chest. "No wonder Christy wants someone to reopen the case. Did you know she was on the phone with her sister when she was shot?"

"Yep. She gave me the gist of the conversation, and I got copies of her sister's case file from NOPD."

"Yeah? What about the sister's phone? Christy said it turned up missing."

"That's right. It was never recovered. Frankly, I think Samhurst blew it, big time. He never should have written it up as a mugging."

"That does seem outrageous. A mugger unloading point-blank into a young girl when any night of the week the Quarter is crawling with drunk guys with full wallets. And what would a mugger want with a phone that could be traced to him?"

Ryker nodded in agreement. "What I don't get, is if the doctor's so all-fired intent on catching her sister's killer now, where was she back then?"

"In Boston, doing her residency or something."

Ryker shook his head. "Think about it. If she'd come home and stirred all this up with NOPD, maybe somebody would have looked at Samhurst's conclusions more closely. It could have saved four young women's lives."

That sick weight in Reilly's chest got a lot heavier. "Yeah. I have a feeling Christy hasn't missed that point."

Ryker nodded grimly. "Okay. I can give you a copy of my files and report. But, kid, I don't know what you think you're going to do—"

Reilly stood. "I'll tell you what I'm going to do. I'm going to find out what happened to Autumn Moser."

Ryker stared up at him. "How exactly? Are you going to go barging into the Eighth Precinct of the NOPD and demand justice?"

"You just get me your reports. And everything you've got on the sister's case."

"Reilly—"

"I may not be a detective, but I'm a law-enforcement

officer. And if I can't do anything through official channels, I'll do it unofficially."

Ryker stood too. "This isn't like you, kid. Tell me you're not trying to get into Christy Moser's—"

"Hey!" Reilly snapped. "Of course not. Come on, Ryker. You saw her. She looks tough as nails on the outside, but she's about to fall apart."

"Well, I definitely saw the tough-as-nails part. And, by the way, the gorgeous part. But falling apart? Nah, she seemed perfectly together to me."

"Well, she's not. Think about it. She's lost her mother and her sister and may lose her father, and now her life is being threatened. She needs someone on her side."

"Okay, Christy Moser's life sucks right now. Why are you getting involved? If she needs protecting, give her the number of Dawson's security agency. She can pay for a bodyguard." Reilly glared at his brother, but before he could open his mouth, Ryker blew out a breath between his teeth. "Don't tell me you've appointed yourself her knight in shining armor?"

Reilly didn't like Ryker's sarcastic tone. "Well," he drawled, "it's not like I'll be the first Delancey twin to do that."

Ryker's lips thinned. "Be careful, Reilly. Don't lose your job over this woman."

"Trust me, old man. If it comes down to my job or her life, it will be an easy choice. I don't intend to let Christy Moser out of my sight until I'm sure she's no longer in danger."

REILLY LEFT RYKER'S office with the Autumn Moser file and headed over to the office of the SWAT commander. He needed to let him know what he was going to be doing, and he didn't want to try to explain over the phone.

Errol "Ace" Acer had been on the St. Tammany Parish SWAT team since its inception in 1980. He'd been SWAT commander for three years. Reilly was one of fourteen officers who, in essence, had two bosses. Mike Davis, the chief deputy of the Chef Voleur office of the St. Tammany Parish Sheriff's Office, and SWAT commander, Acer.

He wanted to get Ace's approval before going through the chief deputy for his request for leave. He drove over to the SWAT leader's office.

"Ace, got a minute?"

Acer looked up, his rugged, lined face grave. When he saw Reilly, a corner of his somber mouth turned up. "Sure, Delancey. Sit."

"Thanks." Reilly didn't want to spend a lot of time chewing the fat with the veteran SWAT officer, although he usually enjoyed it. He needed to get the okay from him and put in his request to Mike Davis before he had to get back to pick up Christy.

Ace stacked the papers he'd been perusing and set them aside with a sigh.

"Problem?"

Ace shrugged one shoulder. "Nothing new. The parents of that kid that shot his buddy over at Ramey Middle School are suing the department."

"Damn," Reilly commiserated. "That was as clean a talk-down as we've ever done."

Ace nodded. "Right. You did a terrific job."

Reilly shook his head. "Everybody did. We were lucky that time."

"Damn straight."

The bottom line of any SWAT team conversation after an incident, whether it was a talk-down or a takedown, was always the same.

We were lucky that time.

Damn straight.

Reilly had never been in a situation that had turned out

"unlucky," which meant that a police officer had been killed. There had only been one incident like that—eleven years ago. One was enough.

"But you're not here to keep me company. What's up?" Ace leaned back in his chair and intertwined his fingers behind his head.

"I want to take leave, and I wanted to ask you first."

"Leave?" Ace's white eyebrows shot up. "Since when? And why are you asking me? Administratively, you're under Mike."

Reilly had never taken any time off, not in the entire four years he'd been on the force. "It's kind of a personal issue," he said. "You're familiar with the October Killer case?"

Ace nodded.

"Moser's daughter is here for the arraignment, and she was attacked last night."

The SWAT commander didn't comment, nor did his expression change. He just waited.

"The attacker told her if she didn't get out of town, she'd be 'as dead as her sister.'" Reilly sat forward. "I want to see if I can help her get her sister's case reopened."

Ace closed his eyes for a moment. "You know that's going to be touchy, since your brother's the primary on her father's case." Typically, he didn't waste words or time. He got straight to the point.

"Yes, sir. Actually, I'm not asking to be excused from SWAT duty. I'll still be on call 24/7. I just wanted to let you know and see if you approved of me taking time from regular duties before I put in my request to Deputy Chief Davis."

Ace sat up. "Sounds good to me. Go for it."

Reilly stood, a little surprised. He'd half expected Ace to react the same way his brother had. But if Ace thought Reilly was being foolish to run off chasing an ice-cold case, he kept his opinion to himself. "Thank you, sir. I'll make sure that Dispatch knows I'm still on call."

Reilly drove back to Chef Voleur and caught Deputy Chief Mike Davis just as he was leaving his office.

"Chief, have you got a minute?"

"On my way to see the sheriff. What is it?"

"I want to take some leave. About a week. Maybe two."

"Leave? Before Christmas?" Mike blinked. "Can Ace spare you from the SWAT team?"

"I talked to him earlier. If you approve, I'll take time from my regular duties but I'll still be available for SWAT duty."

Mike stopped at the door to the parking lot. "What's this about, Reilly?"

Reilly took a deep breath. "Well, sir, I was the first one on the scene at the Oak Grove Inn last night, where a woman was attacked by an unknown assailant."

Mike's eyes narrowed. "Yeah?"

"The woman who was attacked is Albert Moser's daughter. Her attacker told her to get out of town or she'd end up as dead as her sister."

"Moser? The October Killer? Delancey, what the hell are you up to?"

"Sir, she appealed to me to help her find her sister's killer. I want to do that."

"That's an NOPD Detective Division issue, since the girl was killed down in the French Quarter." Mike pushed open the glass door. "Besides, it's a cold case."

"I'm not asking you to approve what I want to do. I'm just asking for time off."

"You're skating on thin ice here, Delancey. I can't defend you if anyone complains."

"Yes, sir. I understand that. Can I get the leave?"

Mike scowled. "I'll have to verify it with Jean-Marie. She's working on the leave schedule for the holidays now. But if you'll agree to work over Christmas, I can probably swing a week right now."

"Thank you, sir."

"Why in hell are you getting mixed up with the October Killer's daughter?"

Reilly didn't see any need to go into detail about *why* he became involved, so he just repeated the facts. "Yesterday, Christy Moser asked me to help her find her sister's killer. Last night she was attacked by someone who threatened her life." He set his jaw and looked at Mike Davis steadily.

"I intend to make sure that the person who got close enough to Christy Moser to threaten her doesn't get that close to her again."

CHRISTY SAT IN THE backseat of the taxi with her head against the seat and her eyes closed, trying to will herself to stop crying. It had been awful the day before, seeing her dad dressed in the ugly orange prison jumpsuit with his hands cuffed in front of him. But as bad as that had been, it didn't hold a candle to seeing him lying in the cardiac care unit, with wires and tubes running everywhere.

Her father was only sixty-two, yet he looked a decade older, if not more. He'd already seemed to age since his first heart attack, which occurred soon after he was arrested. But now, lying so still in that bed, in a mesh of wires and tubes, he looked ancient, shrunken, his complexion nearly as gray as his hair.

His nurse told her they'd sedated him to keep him calm. He reacted when he heard her voice, but he didn't respond. All he did was moan or mutter unintelligibly.

Christy held her breath to keep from sobbing. The man in the cardiac care unit wasn't the man who'd reared Autumn and her, who'd been so strong when their mother had died, who'd celebrated all their achievements and all their special moments with photographs and pages in the big family album he'd kept all their lives.

"Ma'am?"

Christy heard the voice and realized it wasn't the first time she'd heard it. She opened her eyes. It was the taxi driver. The car was stopped.

She squinted through the window. She was here. Her dad's house.

"Oh, thank you," she said as she got out. "Please wait for me."

"Hey, lady. Fares are stacking up. I can't afford to wait. You call the dispatcher when you're ready to go. You owe me thirty-two dollars."

She handed him two twenties. As he pulled away, she reached into her purse and retrieved her key. Thank goodness the officer who'd caught her here the other day hadn't taken it away from her.

She walked up to the door, where new crime-scene tape had replaced the old, and unlocked it. She ducked beneath the tape and entered the house.

The first thing she did was go to the kitchen to look for light bulbs. She was shocked at what she saw. Her dad had never been an excellent housekeeper. He usually ate takeout off paper plates and left them sitting on the kitchen table for days at a time. Often as not, when he made a pan of cornbread, he'd leave the skillet sitting on the stove.

But today, to Christy's shock, everything was spotless. The kitchen table had been wiped and polished. The stove was clean, the sink was empty and there was no old food or grease smell. Even the coffeepot had been cleaned.

A profound sadness shrouded Christy. Her dad had known. He'd known he wouldn't be coming back here. She could imagine him that morning. He'd cleaned up as best he could, because he'd expected to die that day. The day that he lied to her and told her he was making a pan of cornbread for his lunch.

Christy moaned and dropped into a kitchen chair, giving in to a few minutes of helpless sobbing. When she was all cried out, at least for the moment, she got a glass from the cupboard and filled it with tap water and drank. Then she wiped the glass clean and put it back where it belonged. She didn't want to mess up the kitchen her father had cleaned so meticulously. Or telegraph to the police that she'd been there.

Wiping her eyes and pulling in a deep, sustaining breath, she retrieved a box of light bulbs from under the sink, then headed back through the living room and into her sister's bedroom.

She tried the overhead light and the lamp, expecting the bulbs to be burned out, but they weren't. Maybe the police had added new bulbs while they were searching the house. Or maybe her dad had never turned on the lights in Autumn's room since her death.

Christy set the box on Autumn's bedside table, noticing that the police had spread gray fingerprint dust here too. She surveyed the room. The bed had been pulled out from the wall, the drawers of Autumn's dresser were standing open and clothes were piled and scattered, as if careless police hands had rifled through all of them.

Tears welled in her eyes again, but she dashed them away with a swipe of her fingers. She didn't have time to wallow in grief and guilt. She had to get back to the hospital before four-thirty. The rest of her day would go a whole lot easier if Reilly didn't catch her showing up in a taxi, when she was supposed to be there waiting for him.

She looked at Autumn's closet, wondering how thoroughly the police had searched it. Not thoroughly enough, she prayed as she set her purse on the bed and braced herself for the task of searching through her sister's things.

First, she surveyed the racks of clothes and the shelf above the clothing rod. Autumn's taste had always been eclectic, running from black and silver Goth outfits to wild tropical prints and skinny jeans. On the shelf were motorcycle boots sitting alongside sexy, strappy sandals. Her sister's taste in clothes hadn't changed much since Christy had left home when Autumn was sixteen.

She eyed a pile of clothes in the bottom of the closet and wondered if they were Autumn's discards or if they'd been dropped there by the police when they searched. It didn't matter. Not anymore.

Christy pushed the clothes aside and moved a couple of pairs of shoes and a single sock away from the interior wall near the left side of the door. Then she bent down and reached out to slip her thumbnail behind the baseboard.

"Ow," she muttered, pulling her cast-wrapped hand back. Her broken wrist did not want to bend in that direction.

At that moment she heard a car door slam. She froze, not daring to breathe. After a few seconds she heard what sounded like a front door closing, probably across the street. She blew her breath out carefully as she glanced at her watch. She only had about twenty minutes before she needed to get back.

She should have called the taxi back as soon as the grumpy driver left. She had no idea how long it would take to get a taxi out this way. But now that she thought about it, a taxi sitting in front of the house would cause questions. She certainly didn't want the neighbors calling the police to report a suspicious vehicle.

Quickly, she slid farther into the closet on her knees, maneuvering so she could use her left hand to pry the baseboard loose. Christy had never hidden things from her parents. Well, almost never.

But from the moment Autumn could walk, she'd been a pack rat, saving little treasures and secreting them away. She'd been six when she'd discovered the loose baseboard in her closet and the hollow space behind it. She'd shown it to Christy and made her promise never to tell their parents.

Christy never had.

The baseboard fit tightly against the wall. No one would suspect it was loose. Christy slipped her fingernails between the baseboard and the wall and pulled gently. The board gave.

Her heart jumped. *Don't get too excited,* she warned herself. Autumn at six, twelve or even sixteen, hadn't been the same person as Autumn at twenty-one. It could have been years since she'd hidden anything in her secret place. The chance that there might be something there that would give Christy a clue to who had killed her sister was minuscule.

Christy pried the baseboard away from the wall, noting that the adhesive was a piece of chewing gum. *Chewing gum.* She giggled and her heart twisted.

She had to maneuver more before she could slide her hand into the empty space. She cringed, hoping no spiders had taken up residence in her sister's hiding place.

Her fingers immediately encountered a wad of rolled paper. She pulled it out and gasped. Twenty-dollar bills. A lot of them, rolled up and secured with a pink Cinderella ribbon. The sight of the dirty money wrapped with the innocent ribbon was heartbreaking.

"Oh, Tum-tum," she whispered, using the nickname she'd given her sister when Autumn was a baby. "What were you doing?"

Reaching in again, she found a cardboard box. It was barely small enough to fit through the opening, and it took some fancy maneuvering with her left hand to get it out. It was taped up with duct tape. Setting it beside the roll of twenties, she explored the space one more time. In the farthest corner she could reach, she felt some coins and a length of what felt like more ribbon. She pulled them out. The dusty ribbon matched the ribbon used to tie up the bills.

She looked at the coins. Two were Louisiana quarters. But the third disk wasn't a coin at all. It was a button. A brass button, with a few navy-blue fibers attached to it with matching thread.

Christy secured the piece of board back against the wall and crawled out of the closet. When she did, she spotted a cell phone charger plugged into the wall. She grabbed it. Autumn's phone—the phone she'd used to call Christy the night she'd died—had never been found. Christy quickly searched the room, knowing she wouldn't find it. The police had already turned the house upside down. She wondered why they hadn't taken the cord. She looked at it, then put it in her purse, not really knowing why.

She got to her feet and grabbed a tissue out of a box on Autumn's bedside table. She didn't know if it would do any good, since she'd already handled the coins and the button, but she wrapped them in the tissue and stowed it, the box and the roll of twenties in her purse. As much as she was dying to see what was in the box, she knew she needed to get out of there and back to the hospital.

She headed back to the kitchen, set her purse down on the counter, washed her hands and dried them with a paper towel. Then she inspected her clothes. Her pants were covered with cobwebs and dust. Muttering a mild curse, she looked in the junk drawer. A roll of masking tape. Just what she needed. She took a strip of tape in both hands and slid the sticky side along the material of her brown pants, lifting away the dust and cobwebs. As soon as her clothes were halfway presentable, she'd call another taxi.

With any luck, Reilly would never know she hadn't been at the hospital the whole time.

Chapter Five

At four-thirty on the dot, Reilly parked in front of St. Tammany Parrish Medical Center and went inside to pick up Christy. She was nowhere to be found. The waiting room receptionist told him she'd called a taxi.

"Damn it," he muttered, heading back to his car. He should never have left her alone. He should have given her a half hour to sit with her dad and then made her go with him. But after her assault, her dad's heart attack and the grilling Buford Watts had given her this morning, he'd figured she was too upset and exhausted to run off on her own. In fact, she'd almost leaned on him as he'd walked with her to the cardiac care unit earlier. *Almost.*

He'd thought maybe she'd decided that it wasn't so bad having him beside her. Well, she'd shown him. She'd given him the slip the first chance she'd gotten.

Clever, Doc. But not for long.

Hopefully, she'd decided to go back to her room and rest. He headed to the Oak Grove Inn to make sure she was okay. He'd get Ella to check on her, and if she was asleep, he wouldn't bother her. Tomorrow was soon enough to fuss at her for not waiting for him. But a niggling voice in the back of his mind told him Christy Moser was not the type to spend an afternoon in bed.

When he vaulted up the steps of the white clapboard main

house at the bed-and-breakfast, Ella met him at the door, broom in hand.

"Afternoon, Reilly. Watch out."

Reilly stepped back barely in time to miss being coated with the dirt and dust she swept across the threshold.

Once Ella was done, she looked up, past Reilly. "Where's Christy?"

"She's not here?" Reilly asked, not really surprised.

"No." Ella's sharp bird eyes scrutinized Reilly. "D'you lose her?"

He clamped his jaw. "No, I did not lose her." He just didn't know where she was.

Ella gripped her broom like a weapon. "Well, shoo. Get back out there and find her. She doesn't need to be running around on her own. She's hurt and heartsick."

"Yes, ma'am," Reilly said as he backed down the steps, dusting off his pants. Okay, that was a waste of time. Think like her. As he got into his car and cranked the engine, it hit him.

Her dad's house. He muttered a string of curses. Of course. He'd bet six months' pay that she'd taken a taxi to her childhood home. It was still cordoned off as a crime scene, but a few strips of yellow tape wouldn't slow Dr. Christy Moser down a bit.

As he backed out of the B&B parking lot, he speed-dialed Ryker's number to get Albert Moser's address.

When he pulled up to the house, a taxi pulled up behind him. Reilly walked over to the vehicle and handed the guy a couple of twenties.

"Thanks," he said. "You can go on."

The driver shrugged and took off.

Reilly walked up the steps and ducked under the crime scene tape. As he stepped into the living room, Christy hurried out of the kitchen, hiking her purse strap over her shoulder. When she saw him, she stopped and stiffened. "Oh," she said.

"*Oh?*" Reilly crossed his arms and leaned against the foyer wall. "That's what you've got to say? Just *oh?*"

"I—have a taxi coming."

"Not anymore."

She glanced past him at the door then back. "What are you doing here?" Amazingly, she managed to insert a note of righteous indignation into her voice, but the little quaver at the end of the sentence took the starch out of her effort.

"Looking for my damsel in distress." Reilly had to bite his cheek to keep from smiling. She was a tough one all right—on the outside. "The question is what are *you* doing here?"

Her left hand tightened on her purse strap. "I just—I just wanted to see my dad's house. He—" She paused. "He needs his reading glasses."

She was lying. She might as well have been wearing a sign. *I'm a really bad liar.*

"Yeah? He's feeling well enough to read?" he asked mildly.

"Uh, no. Not yet. But I want to make sure he has them when he does feel better." She nodded toward the table next to the big recliner. "They should be—right there, but—" She shrugged. "They're not."

"Maybe the nurses put them with the rest of his things when they admitted him."

"No—" She stopped again, narrowing her eyes at him. "Maybe. I just wanted to help."

There was that note in her voice again. Tough, but underlain with a vulnerability, a note of doubt, as if she wasn't quite sure what exactly she was trying to say. And again, the little quaver at the end. Reilly studied her. Was she on the verge of crying?

He had a feeling she would not appreciate him seeing her

cry. She already resented him for being there to help her when she needed help, whether she would admit it or not.

He longed to take that quaver out of her voice, longed to offer her a shoulder. But she wouldn't accept it or appreciate it. So all he did was step a little closer, close enough that she couldn't ignore him. Close enough to be there if she chose to reach out.

An odd sound came from her. Was it a smothered sob? She was looking down, so he bent his head slightly to meet her gaze.

"It's okay," he said softly. "It's okay to want to see your home. It must not have been easy, coming in here."

Her head shook slowly from side to side, but she still stared at a place on the hardwood floor, not meeting his gaze.

"I'd have brought you," he murmured. "You didn't have to come alone."

"I didn't know he was in such bad shape," she moaned. "I didn't know. I'd have come home. If I'd known he was so sick—I'd have—" Her words got swallowed up by a sob.

Reilly didn't want to make the wrong move, but he couldn't suppress the urge to do something to comfort her. He took a step closer and put a gentle hand on her shoulder.

When he did, she turned toward him. He slid his arm around her and exerted just the slightest pressure. It was enough. She came into his embrace and pressed her face into the hollow of his shoulder. Her breaths were hot against his skin, even through his shirt, and they came in little puffs. She was crying.

It wasn't easy—her crying. It was stifled, bottled-up, pitiful, like a kid trying to hold its breath and cry at the same time. It was obvious Dr. Christy Moser never cried.

"Christy, it's not your fault. What your father did. It's not your fault." He rubbed her back, aware that his resolve to be just a shoulder she could cry on was dissolving fast. Despite his good intentions, he couldn't ignore how sexy her bony, feminine shoulders were. He lowered his gaze to the graceful curve of her neck and the little bump at the top of her spinal column. Even that was sexy as hell.

He swallowed and closed his eyes. "Not your fault," he whispered again and again as he basked in the feel of her slender, supple body pressed against his, and savored the damp warmth of her breath against his skin.

Then, after what could have been a couple of seconds or a dozen minutes, Christy stiffened and pulled away. She turned her back on him and swiped at her eyes with her fingers.

"Excuse me," she said in a muffled voice and headed for the kitchen.

Reilly moved to the kitchen doorway, just to make sure she was all right. And, he had to admit, to be sure she didn't sneak out the back door. She turned on the water tap and splashed her face several times, then pulled a paper towel from a stand to pat her skin dry.

When she turned around, her cheeks were shiny and pink, and her eyes, though rimmed with red, were bright. "Please accept my apology," she said evenly. "This has been a difficult couple of days."

Reilly started to tell her that *difficult* was a mild word for all she'd been through, but he saved his breath. She already knew that.

"Let's go," he said. "You'll want to take a shower and freshen up before dinner."

"I'm not really hungry. I'll probably just ask Ella for a sandwich or—"

"*I'm* taking you out to dinner. You could use a little relief from all the stress and pain of the past few days."

"No, I shouldn't. I ought to go back to the hospital—"

"Hey," he interrupted, placing his fingers lightly against her lips. "You don't get a vote. You're going to dinner with me and that's final. Oh, and I hope you have something casual, because you wouldn't want to ruin your fancy designer pants on the rough wooden seats."

"I don't feel like going out."

He put his hand in the small of her back and ushered her out the front door of her father's house. When he turned to lock the door, her purse bumped heavily against his arm.

"Damn," he said. "What've you got in there? A .38?" As soon as he said the words, a rush of apprehension washed over him. "Tell me you don't have a gun."

"I don't have a gun," she responded.

"How do women walk around with that much stuff hanging off their arms?"

"We're stronger than you think," she said, her mood lightening marginally, although he didn't miss the way her arm tightened around her bag.

Reilly got her settled in the passenger seat of his car and got in on the driver's side and started the engine.

"By the way, Doc," he said offhandedly. "Don't run off without me again. Remember, there's somebody out there that wants you dead."

SEVERAL HOURS LATER, Christy sighed and crumpled the paper towel before tossing it atop the growing pile on the scarred wooden table. "I'm stuffed. I'd forgotten how good boiled crawfish are."

Across from her Reilly grinned, causing sparks to fly from the brightest blue eyes she'd ever seen. She couldn't stop her own mouth from turning up in response.

"That's what you get for running off to Boston," he said, and turned up his mug of beer.

She smiled and shrugged, not letting herself slide back into self-recrimination for leaving her father and sister behind. Reilly had been right. She needed a respite from the stress and grief and guilt. Shrugging again, she commented, "Clams are good too, you know."

He grimaced in mock distaste. "Ugh. Bottom feeders."

"Oh, as opposed to mudbugs?" The nickname for crawfish had come from the crustacean's habit of burrowing into the thick mud of the bayou.

"Mmm," was Reilly's only comment as he popped the head off another crawfish and expertly peeled it and popped the savory bit into his mouth. "Have some more."

"No. I'm really stuffed." She sat back and sipped at her beer, making a face. Beer wasn't her favorite, but Reilly promised her it was perfect with crawfish. It wasn't.

He pulled the bowl of warm lemon-scented water toward them and dipped his fingers, then wiped them off with a clean paper towel.

She did the same. "This is nice."

"Beau's is a really high-class catfish shack."

Christy's mood darkened immediately. "Didn't I see a sign for Henri LaRue Road on the way here?" She'd tried to ignore it at the time, but his mention of the name of the restaurant reminded her.

Reilly's face went solemn. He nodded. "I'm sorry. Maybe I should have taken you someplace else."

"Don't try to snow me, Officer. Henri LaRue Road is where my father tried to kill Nicole Beckham. Did you think I would miss that fact? You chose this place on purpose."

"I didn't, but—" He angled his head without finishing his sentence.

He didn't need to. What he didn't say rang loud and clear. "But there aren't many places around here that don't have something to do with my father's crimes."

"Christy, I—"

She held up a hand. "Just don't. I can deal with it. I have to, until I can get through here and get back to Boston." She turned her palm up in a helpless gesture. "Mandeville, Chef Voleur, Covington, even way out here past Madisonville. My dad really got around, didn't he?"

Reilly looked down at the crumpled paper towel in his hands, then back up at her. "Why did you go to your dad's house?"

Christy felt heat rising from her neck. She took another drink of beer, hoping to quench the fire before it turned her cheeks red. "I told you. I was looking for his reading glasses."

"No, you weren't."

It was irritating how well he could read her. Of course the reading glasses excuse was pretty lame. She could have said a lot of things that would have sounded more plausible. Insurance information. Checkbook. Even underwear.

She couldn't look at Reilly. Damn him and his blue eyes.

"Okay. I felt like I needed an excuse. I just needed to see the house."

He was silent for a moment. "Did it help?"

Christy gave a short laugh. "I don't know. I grew up there. It was just my dad and my sister and me after my mother died. We were—" Her voice gave out. She cleared her throat and tried again. "We were a family. I wanted to see if the house felt the same."

All of that was true, and she could see in Reilly's softening gaze that he believed her—maybe even somehow understood. But it was hard to hold his clear blue gaze, because she was still lying.

Sure, she'd wanted to see the house. But what she wasn't telling him was that she'd wanted to see what was in Autumn's secret hiding place before someone else did. Who knew what was going to happen to the house, now that her father would be spending the rest of his life in jail—*if* he got out of the hospital alive.

If there was any clue to who killed her sister, it would be found in the items she'd pulled from Autumn's closet. Even now, anticipation and fear burned through her. The box was right there beside her, in her purse. She set her jaw and willed herself not to look toward it.

"You ready to go?" Reilly asked.

Christy nodded as she dampened one more towel in the lemon water and cleaned her fingers before picking up her heavy purse.

Reilly guided her through the restaurant and out to his car. Once they were on their way, he said, "How are you dealing with the cast on your wrist?"

Christy looked at it. The edges near her fingers were already becoming grubby. "It's a pain, to tell you the truth. And look how dirty it's getting already."

"What about your wrist. Does it hurt a lot?"

She shook her head. "Not too much. Only if I twist it." She glanced over at Reilly. "I can't thank you enough for the bright pink cast though. It goes with everything."

Reilly laughed. "Wasn't me. I think the EMTs were a little irritated at you bossing them around."

"I'm a physician. I knew what I was talking about."

"And they knew what they were doing. You did get a black eye."

Christy opened her mouth to retort again, then paused, gingerly touching the bruise on her forehead. "Okay. Maybe I deserved a pink cast."

The rest of the drive back to the B&B was pleasant. Reilly talked about mundane things. How the Saints were doing this year, who was slated to appear at Tipitina's on New Year's Eve. His good-natured banter put her at ease and made her feel like an ordinary person out for a nice evening. It was the first time she'd felt normal since she'd arrived back in Louisiana.

She glanced at Reilly sidelong. Again, as when they were eating the po' boy sandwiches, he seemed at ease and comfortable. An ordinary guy on an ordinary date.

It was hard to picture him as a wealthy heir to an infamous fortune.

She needed to believe he was as honorable and caring as he seemed.

When he pulled into the parking lot at the B&B and shut off the engine, she turned to him.

"Reilly, you understand why I had to see the house, don't you?"

He met her gaze. "Sure. It was natural. Illegal, but natural." He sent her a smile.

"No," she said, placing her fingers on his forearm. "I mean you *really* knew. You understood. I could tell." She paused. "Or at least I thought I could." She pulled her hand away. "Okay, sorry. Never mind. I didn't—"

"No, you're right," Reilly said. "When Ryker and I were six, my dad told us that my grandfather was murdered in my grandmother's house. We'd been there before, but after he told us, I couldn't wait to go see it. It was the same place, the same dark halls and countless rooms where we played and ran, but it was different too. I'll never forget how it felt. It was as if—" He stopped and sent her a sheepish glance.

Christy swallowed. "As if evil had taken over? As if it were haunted by the ghosts of the dead?"

Reilly didn't say anything, but he reached out and took her hand. He squeezed it gently. "I'm sorry, Christy. Nobody can possibly know what you're going through, but I'd like to help in any way I can."

His eyes were soft and intense at the same time—a mesmerizing combination. At that moment, she felt as if he could see straight through to her soul.

"Why?" she whispered.

For a long moment he didn't answer. His gaze slid from ers and drifted down to her lips and back up. Was he going o kiss her? A tiny thrill erupted under her breastbone.

Did she want him to?

He met her gaze again. "I don't know," he muttered, sound- ng genuinely bewildered. He blinked, then straightened. "Be- ause that's what knights in shining armor do, I guess." His yes twinkled as he got out of the car and came around to pen the passenger door.

He walked her to the door of the B&B. "So what's on your chedule for tomorrow?" he asked.

Christy thought about the box, the twenties and the button her purse. "Nothing. I'm probably going to sleep in and go ee Dad in the afternoon. I can catch a taxi."

To her surprise, Reilly nodded. "If you can, that would be reat. I've got a few things I need to catch up on."

"Reilly, you don't have to keep spending your time—"

He touched her lips with his forefinger, a gesture that she /as coming to expect whenever she protested. Coming to xpect—and look forward to.

"I know I don't have to. But I'm committed now. You asked ne to find your sister's killer. I intend to do that."

"I thought you were your brother when I said that."

He took a step closer and leveled that intense gaze on her. "But you don't now."

Her mouth went dry. He was so close she could feel the warmth of his breath on her cheek. "No. I don't now."

He leaned forward and brushed his lips across the curve of her jaw, then turned and headed down the steps back to his car.

Shocked, Christy stood there and stared at his back until he got to his car. He turned around and nodded at her with a grin, then got behind the wheel. He cranked the engine, but the car didn't move until she had gone inside the B&B and closed the door.

"No," she whispered to herself. "You're definitely not your brother."

CHRISTY CLOSED THE DOOR to her room and quickly changed into her pajamas and a robe. Then she sat down on her bed and pulled Autumn's treasures out of her purse.

For a long time, she did nothing but sit and stare at them. The box. The twenties. The tissue-wrapped button.

She looked at the box. It was small and square, the kind of box a bracelet or compact might come in, with a textured white surface barely visible under the wrinkled, crooked strips of duct tape. The loose corners of the tape were coated with dust and cobwebs.

Christy got a pair of fingernail scissors from her makeup kit and carefully cut the tape all the way around the edge of the box lid, then with a fearful intake of breath, she opened it.

A folded, crumpled sheet of lined paper, perforated at the top as if it were torn from a small spiral notepad, was the first thing she saw. She lifted it out with the point of the scissors, wishing she had a pair of surgical gloves. If she showed the contents of the box to Reilly—and she wasn't sure she ever would—she didn't want to destroy any evidence.

Under the piece of paper was a small, white plastic bag filled with white powder.

"Oh, my God, no!" she breathed. "Damn it, Tum-tum. Why would you—" She stopped. There was no answer to that question. Her baby sister was dead.

Christy knew what she was looking at. Illegal drugs. What kind, she had no idea, but she'd seen enough television to know what little bags filled with white powder meant. She didn't want to take the chance of puncturing the plastic bag, so she set the scissors down and picked it up by its edge with her fingernails.

On the underside of the bag was a mark. It was smudged, but it looked like a curved *M* or *W* or *3*, depending on which way she turned the bag. And below it was a number, also smudged. Christy didn't even try to decipher it.

The bottom of the little box was dusted with granules of white powder—and there was something else. A tiny plastic rectangle.

Christy started to reach for the scissors, but something about the shape of the little white-plastic rectangle caused her to proceed with caution. With the tip of a nail, she lifted the rectangle. She grabbed its corner and took it out of the box. It was a tiny computerized card, like the SIM cards in cell phones.

Cell phone.

The police had never found Autumn's cell phone. They'd assumed the mugger took it. They'd questioned her and her dad about Autumn's friends, but neither one of them had been able to name a single one. The best Christy had been able to do was to give them the name of Autumn's best friend from high school, but at the time of Autumn's death, Laurie Kestler had been at college in Florida.

Did this SIM card belong to Autumn? It was the kind of thing she'd always kept in her secret hiding place. Her diary, sheets of notepaper on which she'd scribbled the name of her latest crush, cigarettes. If the tiny device held all the numbers Autumn had saved to her phone, it might hold the critical clue to who had killed her.

Suddenly, Christy's fingers were shaking so badly she dropped the card. It bounced from the bed onto the floor, right next to her bare foot. She picked it up. One careless move and she could lose it. As she stared at it lying on her palm, she realized what she needed to do.

She quickly retrieved her cell phone, turned it off and took the back off it. There, peeking out from a slot designed especially for it, was the SIM card for her phone. She started to pry it out with a fingernail, but stopped.

The card in her phone looked larger than the one she held in her hand. It probably wouldn't work. Still, she wanted to try it. As each minute passed, she became more convinced that locked inside that tiny card's even tinier computer chip was the answer to what had happened to her sister.

No. What if she broke the card, or got it stuck in her phone? She had to wait until she could get to a phone store. But in the meantime, what was she going to do with the card? Put it back in the box? She didn't want to do that. She didn't know if the white powder would hurt the card, but she didn't want to take a chance.

She glanced around the room. The décor in the room was a jumbled, eclectic mix of Victorian and American country. One of the Victorian touches was an antique writing desk, complete with feather pen and paper intended to look like parchment. Christy tore a strip of paper and wrapped the SIM card in it, then tucked the little package into the corner of her wallet.

Back at the bed, she stared at the rest of the box's contents. The bag of powder shone as if it were sprinkled with glitter. She rubbed her face tiredly. What was she going to do with it? A part of her wished she had left well enough alone.

Why had she thought it was a good idea to go sneaking into her sister's room and uncovering her secrets? Yes, she'd probably discovered information that could lead to Autumn's killer, but in doing so, she'd come into possession of an illegal substance.

"Damn it, Autumn. How far are you going to go to ruin my life?"

Chapter Six

As soon as Christy muttered the words, she knew they were unfair and self-pitying. Autumn had ruined her own life. She didn't have the power, not even after death, to ruin Christy's.

It was Christy's own fault that she'd gone snooping in her sister's closet. She could have done the right thing and told Reilly or Deputy Watts about Autumn's hiding place. If she had, she'd have nothing to worry about now. She wouldn't be in possession of meth, or heroin, or whatever that white powder was.

She turned her attention to the piece of folded lined paper that she'd taken out of the box, wondering if she should compound her felony by unfolding it and reading what was on it.

She looked toward her cell phone. What she should do is call Reilly and tell him what she'd found. Her face burned at the thought of how he'd react.

Sighing, she turned back to the sheet of paper. She was in too deep already. What could be worse than finding drugs? No. It was never a good idea to think in terms of *what could be worse*.

There were countless things that could be worse. The note could contain the phone number of Autumn's drug connection. Her dealer. A vision swirled through Christy's head—her calling the number, arranging to meet the person and being shot just like Autumn had been, to protect the killer's identity.

Shaking her head at the absurdity of her imagination, Christy decided to unfold the paper. It had been folded twice, so it was a chore to get it unfolded without leaving fingerprints all over it, even when she used the letter opener from the writing desk. But finally it was spread open on the bed.

Christy stared at the words printed there, her brain in a fog as she tried to make sense of them. It certainly wasn't a drug connection. At least, she didn't think it was.

In penciled block letters, the note read, "Hey. Meet me at the shack. I'm 10-10 at 12. Got some stuff for you. B."

Christy didn't know what 10-10 meant. But *shack* and *stuff* sounded ominous. It *could* be a drug connection. Or a love note. Or both. Christy shivered. Her younger sister had been involved in an entire world that was alien to Christy. She had no idea how Autumn had gotten started using drugs in the first place. Christy had been out of high school before Autumn entered. She'd been in medical school by the time Autumn had graduated, so busy with school and labs and rounding with the doctors at the medical center that she hadn't had time for Autumn.

Guilt washed over her again and again she tried to shake it off. She hadn't had a mother or a big sister to guide her in high school, and she'd done fine.

But Autumn had never been as mature as Christy. Or as careful. Had her sister been taken advantage of? Gotten in over her head and found herself addicted before she realized what had happened? Or had she dived in headfirst, the way she'd always taken on any new project or hobby?

Had Autumn made the conscious decision to send her life down the path that had ended with her murder?

Christy rubbed her face again, pressing on her eyelids to

stop their stinging. No matter how it had happened, Autumn's choices had led her to her death, her father to murder and Christy to this point. She had no idea what she was going to do about the note or the drugs, but she knew one thing for sure.

She couldn't leave Louisiana until she found out what had happened to her sister. She hadn't been there for Autumn when it counted, before her death. But now she had a chance to find the person who had murdered her sister. She had Autumn's SIM card. With any luck, the list of saved phone numbers on that card would contain a clue to "B's" identity.

Christy was convinced that this "B," whoever he or she was, knew something about Autumn's death. And Christy was going to find "B" if it was the last thing she ever did.

REILLY SPENT THE BETTER PART of the night in his apartment overlooking Lake Pontchartrain in Chef Voleur, studying the file Ryker had given him on Autumn Moser. She was killed at eleven o'clock at night on October 26, 2005, her twenty-first birthday, in an alley off Basin Street in the French Quarter, near the St. Louis Cemetery.

Reilly shook his head. That area near the St. Louis Cemetery had always been a rough one. The cemetery was the oldest in New Orleans, and its ancient guests were constantly disturbed by drug deals, muggings and killings.

Had Autumn Moser been down there to score, or had she just been in the wrong place at the wrong time? Reilly fanned the pages, looking for Ryker's signed report. He found it in the back.

Ryker had quoted Albert Moser saying that his daughter had a substance-abuse problem. So Autumn could have been down there to buy drugs. He thumbed through the pages until he came to the crime scene photos. The CSI photographer had caught Autumn Moser's face in several shots. Her expression was serene.

Reilly shook his head. She must have lain there unconscious for a while before she died. Her face muscles had had time to relax from the distortion of fear and pain. Her hair was too black and stringy and the overdone dark eye makeup she wore was streaked, but something about the eyes and mouth was very much like Christy.

He kept thumbing through pages, past the CSI statements and the autopsy report, until he got to lead detective Fred Samhurst's typed report.

Cause of death was three gunshot wounds to the chest.
Purse was spilled and her cell phone was missing.

The scrapes on palms and knees and mud spatter on her calves suggest she fell while running. However, the entry wounds place her face-to-face with her killer at near point-blank range.

He flipped back to Ryker's report. There he saw the same questions that had immediately jumped into his own mind. If the mugger were holding her at gunpoint, why had she run? And why had the mugger chased her, caught her and then shot her?

He returned to Samhurst's statement. Detective Samhurst had concluded that Autumn Moser's death was a homicide at the hands of a mugger.

Christy had said she was on the phone with Autumn when she was shot. He flipped a page and found a typed transcription of a phone call Ryker had made to Christy in Boston.

Reilly read through the transcript.

Det. Delancey: I'm Detective Ryker Delancey, St. Tammany Parish Sheriff's Department, Ms.—Dr. Moser. I apologize. I'm calling in regards to your sister's death in 2005. Do you have time to talk for a few minutes?

Dr. Moser: Can you hold a moment?…Now, Detective Delancey is it? I can give you about three minutes. I'm making rounds on the pediatric ward here.

Det. Delancey: I apologize for calling you out of the blue, but I'm looking into your sister's death. I have a statement by you in the NOPD case file on Autumn Moser that states that you spoke with her at 11:00 p.m. on the night of her death.

Dr. Moser: That's right. On the phone.

Det. Delancey: You had called her to wish her happy birthday?

Dr. Moser: Yes. I did.

Det. Delancey: Can you tell me why you called so late?

Dr. Moser: I'd had an emergency with one of my patients and had just gotten home.

Det. Delancey: You reached her on her cell phone. Did she say where she was or who she was with?

Dr. Moser: No. Didn't you say you had my statement in front of you?

Det. Delancey: Yes, I do, but I want to get your perspective about the phone call.

Dr. Moser: She didn't say where she was, but I could hear vehicles and music.

Det. Delancey: You said you heard her scream.

Dr. Moser: Yes. It sounded like she was running, then she stopped and was breathing hard. I asked her if something was wrong. She said, "Christy!" And then she screamed. Then she said something like, "You bum" or "You scum" or something. I heard gunshots. Then the phone went dead.

Det. Delancey: Do you know how many gunshots?

Dr. Moser: Three? Four? I can't be sure. Why are you looking into her case now, after all this time?

Det. Delancey: There have been other murders that may have similarities to your sister's. I want to relook at it in light of these new developments.

Dr. Moser: I see. Have you talked to my father? Albert Moser?

Det. Delancey: Yes.

Dr. Moser: Then you've seen how he has been affected by my sister's death. I'm pleased to know that you're looking into the case, Detective. I hope you're able to do something. My sister's death has ruined my father's health. I have to go now.

Det. Delancey: Thanks for talking to me, Doctor.

The rest of the transcription was contact information, so Reilly went back to Ryker's report. After the phone call to Christy, he had called a friend of his, NOPD detective Dixon Lloyd, and asked him about the lead detective on the Autumn Moser case.

Lloyd had told Ryker that since the murder, Samhurst had suffered a mild heart attack and lost thirty pounds, which had left him forty pounds overweight.

Even though Ryker had told him about Samhurst's weight, Reilly still stared at the numbers. Samhurst had been seventy pounds overweight when he'd caught Autumn Moser's murder case.

As clearly as if they were on the report in front of him, Reilly could see the words Ryker had not written down. *Did Samhurst take the easy way out and write up Autumn Moser's murder as a mugging?*

If he had, he'd contributed to the deaths of four young women and the destruction of two lives, Albert Moser's and his one surviving daughter, Christy's.

CHRISTY WAS JUMPY AND nervous at breakfast the next morning. Ella had cooked a full country breakfast, just as she did every morning, so the table was groaning under the weight of scrambled eggs, sausage and bacon, biscuits, toast, sweet rolls, juice and coffee. Christy pushed scrambled eggs around the plate, holding her fork awkwardly in her left hand as she pretended to listen to Ella's nonstop prattle. The couple from Mississippi happily shoveled food into their mouths. Guerrant, Ella's husband, drank coffee and stared longingly at the newspaper, which was folded neatly on the corner of the large buffet.

As soon as she could, Christy excused herself and rushed back to her room, afraid to leave the incriminating evidence unguarded for even a few minutes. She closed and locked the door behind her and sat down on the bed, her heart racing.

Not only had she become entangled in her sister's illegal activities, she was involving innocent people. Because Christy had brought Autumn's box here, Ella and Guerrant Bardin were technically in possession of illegal drugs on their property.

She unlocked her suitcase and pulled the box out. She set it on the Victorian writing table and stared at it. The fingers of her left hand worried the fraying edge of the cast on her wrist as she considered what she should do.

She should call Reilly. Right now. She shouldn't hold onto the drugs or the note any longer. Every minute she delayed, she was that much deeper into breaking the law. She was a physician in possession of illegal drugs. She could lose her license. Not to mention that she was endangering the Bardins' livelihood.

She picked up her phone, then hesitated. Reilly was busy. He'd told her he had something he needed to do today. And he hadn't told her to call him if she needed him, the way he had the night she was attacked.

She didn't want to call him in the middle of a meeting, or if he were involved in police business. He'd contact her as soon as he could. She knew that.

For whatever reason, Reilly had appointed himself her personal guardian. He wouldn't waste any time getting back to her.

When he did, she'd tell him everything. Or almost everything, anyhow.

She slid her phone back into her purse. While she waited to hear from Reilly, she was going to take her rental car and go find a cell phone store. She wanted to see the numbers on that SIM card, numbers Autumn had thought were important enough to keep in her secret hiding place.

Christy locked the box inside her suitcase and draped a scarf casually over it. If anyone disturbed her suitcase, she'd know by the position of her scarf. Then she quickly dressed and, after locking the door to her room, headed out to her rental car. It wasn't as easy to drive as she'd hoped it would be, but at least she was able to handle the steering wheel and the automatic shift without too much pain or trouble, even with the cast on her right hand.

At the first cellular store she found, she showed the SIM card and the charger cord to the clerk, who told her the phone that took that cord used a larger SIM card.

So the phone Autumn had been using that fatal night was not the same phone the hidden SIM card had come from. The clerk sold Christy a phone that used the same card and all its accessories, including a fully charged battery that Christy talked him into giving her. She could not wait for the battery to charge overnight.

She sat in her car and went through the saved numbers on the card. There were the usual contact numbers for the cellular service plan, Triple A Wrecker Service, a doctor's office, a pharmacy and a pizza delivery service. The only names that meant anything to her were their dad's, of course, Christy's own cell phone number and a number for Laurie Kestler, Autumn's best friend from high school.

Christy breathed a little sigh of relief that Autumn still had Laurie Kestler's number. At least she could talk to one person who had known Autumn. That is, she could try. After all, the numbers listed on the card were at least five years old.

She hoped and prayed Laurie could tell her who the other names were. Or at least some of them. From what she remembered of Laurie, she doubted the girl would know anyone called *Slick* or *Jazzy* or *Glo*. But maybe she'd be able to identify *Jeff, Tina, Frankie* or *D.B.*

D.B. Could that be the "B" who'd written the note Autumn had hidden in her box? Christy's pulse raced as she looked at the number. It was a local area code. She could just call—see who answered.

Her thumb hovered over the call button, but she hesitated. If someone did answer, what would she say? *Hi there. I think you know something about my sister's murder?*

After staring at D.B.'s number for a moment, she moved her thumb away from the call button and pressed the Down arrow until she got to Laurie.

She dialed it.

"Hello?" a soft voice answered.

"Laurie? This is Christy Moser, Autumn's sister."

There was a slight hesitation. Christy was probably the last person Laurie had ever expected to hear from.

"Um, yeah? Hi?"

"I'm sorry to bother you, but I found your number in Autumn's things and I wanted to ask you a few questions. Do you have time to talk for a minute?"

"I guess," she said hesitantly. "I just put the baby down for a nap."

"The baby?" That surprised Christy. She'd been picturing

Laurie as still twenty-one, like Autumn. "How lovely. Congratulations. Boy or girl?"

"She's a girl. Aynsley. She's three months old." Laurie paused. "Um, my mom told me about your father. I—"

"That's all right, Laurie. I need to find out if you know any of these names." She read the list of names from Autumn's SIM card.

"I—don't think so," Laurie said.

"I know it's been five years, but please think. Are you sure none of the names sound familiar?"

"I didn't know most of the people Autumn hung out with there at the end. We didn't talk much after she got into all the drugs. I'm—I'm sorry."

"Don't worry about it. I know what Autumn was doing. I know she was into drugs. So you can't figure out who Glo is? Spelled G-L-O? Or the initials D.B.?"

"There was a guy named Danny that graduated with us. He had a crush on Autumn, but I don't think his last name started with a B."

"Do you remember anything else about him?"

"No. He played soccer, I think."

"What about a boyfriend? Did you know who Laurie was seeing?"

"I really don't want to—"

"Laurie, listen to me. You're not going to hurt my feelings and you're not betraying Autumn's confidence. You'll be helping us find her killer."

"Okay, but please. I don't want to get into trouble. I should have told the police this back then, but I was in Florida, and they never talked to me."

Christy felt her pulse fluttering in her throat. Maybe Laurie did know something that would lead to Autumn's killer.

"It's okay, Laurie. I *swear* you won't get into trouble." As she finished speaking, Christy heard a baby crying.

"Oh, no, the baby's awake." Christy heard movement through the phone. Laurie must be heading for the baby's room.

"Laurie, just two minutes, please. Tell me what you know."

The girl sighed. "Autumn bragged to me that her boyfriend could get her stuff—you know."

Christy did know. *Stuff* equaled *drugs*.

"Did she tell you anything about him?"

"He was married, and she used to say that he had to protect his reputation and his job. It was like she was proud that he had to keep her a secret."

The baby's crying got louder. Laurie was in the baby's room now.

"I really have to go," Laurie said, then whispered cooing baby words.

"All right. Thanks, Laurie." Christy sighed as she hung up. Not much help. Of course, she hadn't expected much. From what she remembered about Laurie, she could have predicted that Autumn's high school friend wouldn't know Autumn's newer—probably drug-using—friends.

But the bit about the mystery boyfriend was interesting. He had to protect his reputation and his job. What could that mean? Was he a politician? A well-known businessman? The possibilities were endless, unless Autumn was just bragging.

As for Autumn's friends, she had more of a lead than before. Maybe if she could find a yearbook from Autumn's senior year, she could figure out who Danny was. Or even Glo or Jeff.

A phone ringing startled her. For an instant she thought it was the new phone—maybe Laurie calling back. But then she realized it was hers. She looked at the display.

Reilly.

She pressed her lips together as she answered.

"Where are you?" he demanded before she even had a chance to say *hello.* "And please tell me you're not driving your rental car."

"Hi to you too," she threw back at him.

"Christy—"

"I decided to try driving, and what do you know? I can drive just fine." She flexed her right fingers and a pain shot along the back of her hand. She winced.

"I thought you said you were going to take a taxi to see your dad."

"As I just said—"

"So are you at the hospital now?"

"No. I haven't made it over there yet."

"You haven't made it over there. Back to my original question," he growled. "Where are you?"

"On my way back to the inn." She swallowed, pressed her lips together again, then continued. "Can you meet me there? I need to show you something."

There was a pause on the other end. "Tell me you didn't go back to your dad's house."

"I didn't go back to my dad's house today," she said carefully.

She heard Reilly sigh. "Thank goodness. I'll see you at the inn."

Christy hung up and started the car. But her gaze strayed back to the new cell phone. It would be so easy just to call one of those numbers. Yes, whoever she called would be a stranger, but she could tell them that she was looking for a friend of her sister's.

What could it hurt? She picked up the phone and ticked through the stored numbers until she got to D.B. Her thumb hesitated over the call button, but finally, with a deep, fortifying breath, she pressed it.

The phone rang so long she figured it would go to voice mail. When she finally heard a click, she waited, holding her breath, to hear what the message said.

But what she heard wasn't a prerecorded message. After an infinitesimal pause, a voice said, "Who is this?" The question was a cross between a growl and a whisper, definitely male. Was he trying to disguise his voice? If so, that meant whoever was on the other end of the phone thought the caller might recognize him. Laurie's words echoed in her head.

He had to protect his reputation and his job.

She forced air into her lungs. "Is this D.B.?"

The voice lowered in pitch. "Who is this?" he repeated menacingly.

"I'm Christy Moser. I found this number in my sister's phone." Not strictly true, but simpler than trying to explain about the SIM card.

She heard a sharp intake of breath, then the phone went dead. She called back, but that time the phone went straight to a digitized female voice reciting a generic message.

"We're sorry, but the owner of this number has not yet set up a voice mailbox. Please call again."

What if the number was one of those pay-as-you-go phones? If the man who had answered was D.B., would he throw the phone away?

Apprehension grew in Christy's chest. Had she just made a fatal mistake?

Had she just talked to Autumn's killer?

Chapter Seven

After spending the night going over Ryker's file on Autumn Moser, Reilly had planned on sleeping late. If he was up by nine o'clock, he'd have plenty of time to get to an official dress-uniform press conference at the mayor's office.

But at a quarter to six, a call had come in for the SWAT team to respond to a situation at a convenience store. A kid had gone in to rob the store, and had ended up holding the clerk and a female customer at gunpoint. It had taken three hours to talk the kid out.

As Ace had commented afterward, they'd been lucky that time.

Reilly barely made it to the mayor's press conference on time. He'd had no chance to change clothes prior to heading down to the police station on Royal Street to pick up the original Autumn Moser case file. Even though he'd called ahead, he'd had to wait over an hour while the file clerk found it, enduring good-natured ribbing about walking around in his dress blues.

By the time he'd made it back to the inn and discovered that Christy and her rental car were gone, it was nearly four.

He was forced to listen to Ella talk about her nephew, who'd been in trouble with the law but who was a good kid, while he waited for Christy. He nodded and smiled and made the appropriate responses at the appropriate times, all the while swearing he was going to make Christy pay for that twenty-five minutes he'd never see again.

Finally he heard a car pull into the parking lot. Through the glass panes of the front door he saw Christy. She managed to look perfectly at ease as she strode up the walk, although he did notice that the knuckles of her left hand were white where she gripped the strap of her shoulder bag.

Excusing himself from Ella with a comment about official business, he stepped out onto the porch and closed the front door behind him.

"Glad you could make it," he said.

She looked up, then did a double take. "Wow! You're in uniform," she said.

"Yeah. It's been a busy day."

Something about how he looked or what he said bothered her. Her hand tightened even more on the straps of her shoulder bag, and she was staring somewhere in the vicinity of his uniform pocket.

"Apparently it has been for you too. Where have you been?"

She sent him an irritated glance. "I have something I need to tell you—to show you."

Reilly heard the undertone of apprehension, maybe even fear, in her voice. "Okay," he said, glancing back at the front door. He could see a distorted silhouette through the beveled glass. Ella. "Let's go some place where we can talk."

"It's—I need to get something out of my room."

Reilly nodded and opened the front door. "Hurry," he said for Ella's benefit. "We're already late for that appointment."

Christy shot him a questioning glance. He stared at her, willing her to understand that he didn't want to get embroiled in another gab-fest with Ella.

Her gaze flickered and she nodded. "I know," she responded. "I'll hurry." She unlocked her door, slipped inside and closed it firmly.

Reilly glanced over at Ella, who had her mouth open, about to speak.

"Official police business," he said. "Urgent. No time to talk."

Ella's black eyes sparkled and her cheeks turned pink. "Oh, what's it about?" she breathed.

"That's classified," he snapped officiously.

Ella pursed her lips, but her eyes still sparkled. She turned and practically ran toward the back of the house. Going to tell Guerrant that she'd been involved in *official police business*. Reilly blew out a breath. Anything to stop her talking.

When Christy emerged, locking her door behind her, she had that death grip on her purse and her face was pale.

He didn't ask any questions. They got into his car and drove to his condo.

As they got on the glass elevators and he pressed the button for the eighth floor, Christy looked a little taken aback. "What is this?" she asked.

"My apartment. I figured we could talk here without anyone disturbing us."

She nodded, but sent him a narrow glance. A suspicious glance.

Not exactly the response he normally got on the rare occasions he brought a date home with him. The address alone generally had them squirming with lust and greed. And that turned him off. Therefore, he'd be hard-pressed to remember the last time he'd invited a woman up here.

He'd bought the condo because it was easy, not because it was impressive or because he enjoyed flaunting the money he'd inherited from his grandparents. But women generally insisted on being impressed. The condo had turned into an excellent tool for measuring women's reactions. The more impressed they were the less interested he was.

So Christy's reaction intrigued him. He unlocked his door and entered first. He wanted to gauge her reaction when she saw where and how he lived.

Christy stepped into the living room, her gaze immediately going to the glass wall that overlooked Lake Pontchartrain. The sun was setting, and red and gold light sparkled on the lake's restless waters and turned the buildings into silhouettes. He knew it was a breathtaking sight.

She stared at it for a few seconds, then slowly turned her gaze to the rest of the room.

After he'd moved in, Reilly had asked his cousin if she'd pick out some furniture for him. Cara Lynn had done a good job. She'd bought leather and wood—pieces with clean lines and sturdy construction. Like the apartment, the furniture was designed for ease and comfort.

"Nice apartment," she said. "Comfortable."

"Thanks," Reilly said, surprised again. Not only was she not drooling over the address or the view, she seemed to get why he liked it. He scrutinized her as she stepped farther into the room.

"Do you cook?" she asked, checking out the chef's-grade gas stove, the vented grill, the zero-degree refrigerator-freezer and all the kitchen accessories.

"No," he laughed. "I wield a mean can opener though. And I'm particularly proficient at calling for pizza."

She smiled. "That's a waste of a great kitchen."

"Yeah, it came with the place. What can I say?"

She seemed fairly at ease, but he didn't miss the fact that she hadn't loosened her hold on her purse one bit.

He moved to stand beside her. Just as he opened his mouth to ask her what she had to show him, his cell phone rang.

"Excuse me," he said to her, then looked at his phone. It was Commander Acer.

"Delancey," he said.

Ace asked him if he'd finished his report before he left.

"Yes, sir. I apologize, sir. I left it in the printer."

"No problem. I'll get it. 10-4."

"Yes, sir. 10-4." When he hung up and turned, Christy was staring at him, all color gone from her face.

"What's the matter?" he asked.

She didn't answer for a couple of seconds. "I—I'm sorry. I'm just really tired." She looked past him, out at the lake, then back. "Did you say 10-4?"

"Yeah." He smiled. "Just like in the cop shows. Why?"

"What does it mean?"

"It's police code. It basically means *message received and understood*."

"Oh, right. I think I've heard that on TV, haven't I?"

She wouldn't look at him. He couldn't figure out what had just happened, but while he was on the phone with Ace, Christy's body language had gone from displaying relative calm to spine-cracking tension. What had changed? He watched her carefully as he went on.

"The cop shows love to use them. You'll hear 10-4 a lot. And 10-20 for location. You've heard them ask, 'What's your twenty?'"

"Oh, right." She paused then met his gaze. "Haven't I heard of 10-10 too?"

"Yeah. 10-10 stands for off duty. Nobody really uses them much anymore. A few of the older guys. But there are dozens of codes. Too many to remember."

"I see," she said in a brittle voice. Her shoulders drew up and she dropped her gaze. "Would you mind if I used your bathroom?"

Reilly pointed. "Right back there. There's a half bath at

the end of the hall." As she disappeared he went over the last few moments in his mind.

Something had upset her—suddenly and badly. Was it his short conversation with Ace? They hadn't spoken a dozen words.

She'd asked him about the ten codes, but was that just a diversion, to try and keep him from guessing what was really bothering her?

CHRISTY HADN'T ALLOWED herself to think about anything except walking calmly and confidently until she got inside the guest bathroom and closed the door.

As soon as the latch clicked into place, Christy let out her breath in a whoosh and sat down on the closed toilet lid. Her legs were quivering so badly she wasn't sure she could have stayed on her feet. And she felt nauseated.

So 10-10 meant off duty. As soon as Reilly had said 10-4 on the phone she'd realized she'd heard numbers like that before, on police shows on television. Police shows. *Police.*

Dear God, the man Autumn had been seeing was a police officer. Christy's mouth went dry and her stomach did a double backflip.

Yesterday when she'd found the drugs in Autumn's hiding place, she'd admonished herself for thinking that nothing could be worse than finding drugs. And this was why. There was always something that could be worse.

Of all the people Autumn could have been seeing, a cop was the absolute worst. Everything she'd heard about the mystery man began to make sense. Laurie saying that Autumn told her he had to protect his reputation and his job. Her father declaring that Autumn's boyfriend was afraid of jeopardizing his job.

Christy realized she was panting. Hyperventilating. She put her hands over her mouth. "Oh, dear God," she whispered.

A cop. That explained the brass button too. It was just like the ones she'd noticed on Reilly's dress uniform.

She had no idea what she was going to do. She'd thought she was in trouble when she found the little bag of drugs. But now, she had evidence that Autumn's boyfriend, the man who may have been supplying her with drugs, the man who may have killed her, was a law-enforcement officer.

She had to tell Reilly.

No. She couldn't tell Reilly. He probably knew the man. Besides, she had sense enough to know that a note and a button wouldn't stand up against a department full of cops. She knew about the "blue line." This wouldn't be the first time her family had been on the wrong side of the line that separated civilians from police.

Quickly, aware that she'd been in the bathroom for several minutes, Christy pulled the box out of her purse and opened it. She picked up the note with her fingernails and stuck it down into her wallet, then closed the box.

She'd show Reilly the drugs and the roll of twenties. If she were very lucky, maybe there were fingerprints all over them, implicating whoever had given them to Autumn. If not, well, she'd just have to come up with more proof.

She rinsed her fingers and splashed a little water on her face before going back out to face Reilly.

He was waiting for her, looking concerned. His intense blue eyes searched hers. "Christy, what's wrong?" he asked.

"Wrong?" She looked at him questioningly.

He arched a brow and his expression clearly said, *Give me a break.* Then he touched her left hand.

She looked down and saw that she had that death grip on her purse again. She consciously flexed her fingers and took a deep breath.

"I wasn't telling the truth about why I went back to Dad's house," she said.

He took her hand and squeezed it. "Relax. I know you weren't. Tell me why you really went back there."

"I needed to check something. To find something." She pushed her hair back with her right hand, and a few hairs caught in the pink cast. "Ow," she muttered, jerking her hand away.

"Here," he said, guiding her over to the leather sofa. "Sit down and try to relax. I'll get you something to drink. What do you want?"

She shrugged. "What do you have?"

"Just about anything. That's a big refrigerator."

"Cranberry juice?"

"Yep." He fetched her a bottle of cranberry juice and himself some water. As she took the bottle, he glanced at his watch. "Are you hungry?"

She shook her head automatically. It was obvious she needed to get whatever was bothering her off her chest as soon as she could. He'd call for pizza later, or scramble some eggs. That much he could do.

"Okay, so you went to your dad's looking for something?"

She looked miserable, sitting there on his tan leather sofa with her purse in her lap. She held on to it with both hands, as if afraid he was going to grab it away from her.

"Autumn was never a very trusting person," she said. "She hid things—her favorite treasures, her secret notes. You know, like a kid will."

He waited, knowing she had to start like this. He'd talked to desperate people, grief-stricken people, angry and hurt and terrified people, in his experience on the SWAT team. They rarely told their stories in a straightforward manner. They all were tormented by their experiences, their memories, and they had to let it out somehow. In his time working on the SWAT team, taking his turn as lead negotiator, he'd become a very good listener.

"She was so young when our mother died. Only twelve. It hit her hard. I was older. More mature."

By four years, Reilly thought. Not so much older.

"Autumn had a secret hiding place in her closet, behind a loose baseboard. I was sure the police hadn't found it. I was right." Christy stared at her hands for a long time without speaking.

"So you went there to see if Autumn had left anything in her secret hiding place?" he asked, his voice prodding gently.

"I found a roll of twenties—a big roll," she said, glancing up at him briefly before continuing. "And a box."

There it was. The answer to why she was so protective of her purse. That's what had her so spooked. She needed to tell him about what she'd found. She needed to show it to him, but she was terrified.

"Do you have the box and the roll of bills with you?" he asked.

She nodded.

"Can I see them?"

It took her a few seconds to force her fingers to let go of her purse, but she finally pulled out the roll of twenties and set it on the large glass coffee table. Then she dug into her purse again and came up with a small rectangular box. It was crudely taped up with duct tape.

Reilly waited until she'd set the box on the coffee table. Then he spoke. "Can I look at the box?"

She raised her green eyes to his and he thought of a rabbit watching a hawk diving toward it. His heart twisted. He couldn't imagine what was in the box that had her so spooked.

No, that wasn't true. He *could* imagine what was in it. All too easily. From what he'd read about Autumn, the girl had been deep into drugs. So he was pretty certain, based on how Christy was acting, that he knew exactly what was inside the box. He just hoped he was wrong.

She nodded, and her tongue flicked out to moisten her lips. Her throat moved as she swallowed.

He picked up the box and pulled on the lid. A couple of pieces of duct tape tried to stick, but he peeled them back. He looked inside.

Damn it. A bag of white powder. Exactly what he'd expected. Exactly what he'd hoped he wouldn't find.

"I'm sorry," Christy whispered.

Reilly set the box and lid down. He was furious. Furious and afraid—for Christy. "When did you find this?" he asked evenly.

She swallowed. "I told you, yesterday."

"You had it in your purse when I got to your dad's house."

Her gaze faltered and she nodded.

"It was in your purse when we went to dinner last night?"

"No," she muttered. "It was in my room."

"So you found this at—what—three in the afternoon? We were together all evening, and you didn't think it was worth mentioning?" He could hear the ice-cold fury in his voice, and he didn't miss the growing fear in Christy's body language.

Her fingers were bluish-white from clutching her purse. Her shoulders were tight and stiff and he could detect a fine trembling throughout her entire body.

"Christy, do you know what this is?"

She started to speak, faltered then cleared her throat. "Of course I do." Her voice was brittle.

"Why in hell—" He stopped. It didn't matter why she

hadn't called the police or told him earlier. He had to deal with it now.

"We've got to turn this in."

She nodded.

He put the top back on the box. Then he went to the kitchen and grabbed a plastic grocery bag and put the box and the roll of twenties into it.

Christy hadn't moved.

Reilly sucked in a deep breath. He didn't want to ask the next question, because he wasn't sure he wanted to see how bad a liar Dr. Christy Moser was. Nor did he want the knowledge her lie would give him. But he had to ask. "So, is this everything?"

She glanced up at him questioningly.

"Did you find anything else?"

She opened her mouth but nothing came out.

"What else did you find, Christy?"

She swallowed. "Some ribbon. A few coins."

"Is that all?"

"Reilly, I—"

"Is. That. All."

She looked down at her hands and nodded.

"What about the bag. Did you touch it?"

"Just with my fingernails."

"The inside of the box?"

Her shoulders slumped. "Probably."

"Okay. You found this stuff yesterday and brought it back to your room at the inn, but you didn't open it until this afternoon, and you called me as soon as you saw what was in it."

"No, I—?"

He stopped her with a raised hand. "Listen to me. You did not open the box until this afternoon and you called me right away. You only touched the contents enough to see what they were."

"Are you sure—?"

"Trust me, Christy, you don't want to explain why you kept it for more than twenty-four hours before you told anyone about it."

"Okay." She stood.

"And Christy, I need to be sure, before I take this to the police, that there's not something else I should be giving them."

She shook her head—too quickly, too hard.

He bit his tongue to keep from pressing her. There had been something else in that hiding place. He'd bet his condo on it. But he had to get the drugs and money to the sheriff's office—now. So he was happy to accept her answer at face value, although deep in his heart he knew she was lying.

THEY SPENT THREE HOURS at the sheriff's office while the deputy on duty processed the evidence and took their statements.

The first thing the deputy did when he saw the bag was take a pair of tweezers from his desk drawer and pick it up to examine it. "Did anyone touch this?" he asked.

Reilly nodded at Christy.

"I touched it with my fingernails, but that's all."

While she was talking, the deputy turned the bag over to look at the bottom. "I'll be damned," he breathed.

"What?" Reilly leaned forward.

"That's an evidence marker." The deputy pointed at the smudged letter on the bottom of the plastic bag. "If I'm not mistaken, it's Amber Madden's mark. She's one of the crime scene analysts."

Reilly squinted at the mark and uttered an expletive.

Christy's heart leaped in a combination of fear and

excitement. "What does that mean?" she asked, although she was pretty sure she knew.

Reilly and the deputy locked gazes for an instant. The deputy cleared his throat. "Well, it looks like this bag was logged into evidence. That number identifies the case file."

A pang of fear stabbed Christy deep in her chest. Whoever Autumn was involved with had given her drugs stolen from police evidence. It had to be someone in the sheriff's department.

That information drove home the seriousness of what she was doing. She was withholding evidence. Evidence that could lead to the man who killed her sister.

Reilly scrutinized the mark and the number. "Do we have any reports of missing evidence? This had to have been at least five years ago. The girl who hid this box was killed in 2005."

"This number underneath will identify the case," the deputy said. "We'll know soon enough. To answer your question, there are always a few instances of missing evidence."

"But drugs," Reilly insisted. "Wouldn't that have been investigated?"

Reilly and the deputy exchanged a glance, and then the deputy's gaze flickered toward her.

She looked down at her lap. The deputy was already regretting talking about missing evidence in front of her. Reilly obviously agreed because he sat back in his chair and looked at his watch.

"Anything else, Deputy?" he asked.

The deputy rolled his chair back from the desk. "We'll need to get your fingerprints, Dr. Moser."

He explained to her that they were needed to exclude her from any suspect fingerprints they found on the bag. He got her to give him a crude drawing of the exact location of Autumn's secret hiding place, and interrogated her about other possible hiding places in the house. He explained to her that since the house and lot were still classified as a crime scene, they wouldn't need any additional paperwork to search them again. She signed a statement indicating that she understood.

Finally they were free to go. The money and the box with its contents stayed at the precinct, and the deputy promised to let Reilly know what came of the search of Albert Moser's house.

Reilly and Christy made the drive back to the Oak Grove Inn in silence. He walked her to the door. "I'll call you in the morning," he said. "Can I trust you not to go running off in your car?"

Her eyes sparked with irritation as she nodded. "Yes," she said stiffly, turning the glass knob on the door.

He took a step backward.

She turned back toward him. "Reilly, I'm sorry—" She stopped, her eyes sparkling with unshed tears.

He had an odd urge to pull her into his arms and tell her everything was okay, but the urge wasn't quite as strong as the anger that still burned in his chest. Anger that she hadn't confided in him about finding the box. Anger that she had put herself in jeopardy by holding on to illegal drugs. Anger that she didn't trust him enough to tell him what else she'd found.

And yet, he couldn't stop himself from touching her cheek. "Good night," he said evenly. "I'll watch until I see your lights come on. Try to get some sleep."

After she went inside and closed the front door behind her, he headed back to his car. But he didn't crank the engine until she turned on the lights in the front guest room.

As he put the car in Reverse, the unmistakable crack of a gunshot split the night, followed by the sound of breaking glass and a short, piercing scream.

Chapter Eight

Before the scream had died down, Reilly had his phone in his hand. "Dispatch, Officer Delancey here. Need backup at Oak Grove Inn, Covington. Shots fired."

Then he grabbed his weapon and his high-powered flashlight from his glove compartment and jumped out of the car. He sprinted toward the side of the house from which the rounds had come. He held the flashlight in his left hand and used his left wrist to support the weapon held in his right. He reached the wall and flattened his back against it. He sidled toward the corner.

He heard the front door open. He glanced back. It was Guerrant.

"Get back inside and take cover," he stage-whispered.

He hoped to hell Christy was okay.

Once he reached the corner of the house, he took a deep breath and darted his head out, then back immediately. He didn't see anything that looked human. So more slowly, he rounded the corner, leading with his weapon balanced atop the flashlight.

Once he stepped out of the shelter of the house, motion-activated floodlights flared, illuminating the side yard. He scanned the area, looking for anything odd. Anything that moved.

He examined the ground below the window where thick,

springy grass grew. There would be no way to get a shoe print.

Beyond the fence was the vacant lot he'd gotten a glimpse of the other night, when Christy was attacked. It was a tangle of overgrown hedges, vines and bramble bushes. Sweeping the area with his flashlight beam, he noted that several yards past the fence, the bushes turned into trees.

Whoever had fired the shot could easily have escaped through there. But not without some scratches. He filed that information away to give to the responding officers.

For an instant, Reilly thought about trying to give chase, but it had been at least twenty seconds since the shot was fired. The shooter was probably far gone by now.

He aimed the flashlight toward the back of the house, then toward the parking lot, but nothing seemed out of place. He switched off the light and pocketed it, but kept his weapon ready as he headed back around the front of the house.

When he turned toward the front door, he saw Guerrant standing on the porch with his shotgun. Would Guerrant hesitate to use the weapon if he were threatened? Given his calm expression and the ease with which he held the gun, Reilly was pretty sure the owner of the inn would have no trouble unloading both barrels if the situation warranted it.

"Backup's coming," he told Guerrant as he ran up the steps. "Tell them the shooter went through the vacant lot."

Guerrant nodded. "I already talked to the folks in the cottages."

Reilly ran inside. Christy's door was open. Ella's voice, an octave higher than normal, came from inside.

"Christy!" he shouted as he ran into the room.

Christy was sitting on the edge of the bed, white as a sheet. When she saw Reilly, she started to rise, but Ella, who was fluttering around her like a mother hen, pushed her back down.

"Don't get up, dear. You'll faint." Ella looked over her shoulder at Reilly. "Oh, my goodness," she cried. "What in the world is going on out there?"

Reilly barely acknowledged Ella. He was worried about Christy. "Are you okay? You're not hurt are you?" he asked her.

She stared at him, eyes wide. Her lips were pinched and white at the corners, and her hands were clenched together in her lap.

Reilly started toward her, but was stopped by Ella, who wailed, "Those windows were the original glass."

She gestured wildly at the broken glass, then turned back to Christy. "Oh, my God, you could have been killed."

"Ella," Reilly snapped. "Go make some coffee."

"Oh, my God," the woman said again. "We're going to be up all night." She hurried out of the room. "I'd better make some coffee," she said, as though she hadn't heard him.

As soon as Ella was gone, Christy stood and came to Reilly.

He put his arms around her and hugged her, then pushed her to arm's length with gentle hands on her shoulders.

Tears glistened in her wide, frightened eyes, and one slipped down her cheek.

He stopped it with a finger. She looked unhurt, but her pallor worried him. "Are you sure you're okay?"

She nodded. "I'm not injured. However, I do seem to be having a mild—panic attack." Her breath came in little puffs and she pressed her left hand against her breastbone. "It's so silly how the reaction doesn't set in until after the danger is over."

Her effort to diagnose herself logically, coupled with the indignant note in her voice made him feel much better. He'd hated seeing her terrified and unsure of herself. He knew she hated being that way.

He smiled wryly. "Yeah," he said. "Silly. I'm glad you're not hurt. Tell me what happened. Were you standing at the window?"

"No. I was right there—" she gestured "—in front of the dresser, taking off my watch and jewelry."

Reilly measured the distance between the dresser and the window with his eyes. At least four feet. He walked over to the window. The house was on a traditional foundation, a couple of feet off the ground, so the shooter had to have his back against the fence to aim at Christy where she'd stood in front of the dresser.

"Why in hell would anybody put lacy curtains and nothing else on a bedroom window? There ought to be shades or blinds on these windows." He inspected the broken pane, then turned and walked to the other side of the room and swept the wall with his gaze. Sure enough, about two feet above his head, a bullet was embedded in the wallpaper.

"I guess blinds aren't authentic."

"What?" he asked distractedly as he turned back to look at the window. The trajectory would have put the bullet about a foot behind Christy.

"Blinds," Christy said. "Maybe shades were used back in Victorian times, but blinds probably weren't."

He looked at her, frowning, then realized she was answering his rhetorical question about the curtains.

"Oh, right," he said. A little color was coming back into her cheeks as she calmed down. So he decided not to tell her how narrowly the bullet had missed her.

He turned his attention back to the window. Had the gunman been shooting to kill? Or had the shot been a warning? A second warning to Christy to go back to Boston and forget about trying to find out who had killed her sister.

"It almost hit me, didn't it?" Christy asked, her voice small. "I thought I felt something swish by me." She shivered.

Reilly realized she'd been watching him carefully. She hadn't missed his mental calculations of the bullet's trajectory.

"I don't think he was trying to kill you," he said, hoping he sounded reassuring.

"Why not? He told me he would. Assuming it was the same man who attacked me. If you're just trying to make me feel better, don't."

"Okay," he said. "I didn't check while I was outside, but with those ridiculous curtains and the lights on in here, I'm pretty sure he could see you clearly. If he's any kind of decent shot, he could have killed you if he'd wanted to."

He regretted his honesty when the returning color faded from Christy's cheeks.

"Let's go to the dining room. I called for backup. They'll be here any minute."

As soon as the words were out of his mouth, he heard the sirens coming rapidly toward them. "There they are."

He led her through the front parlor and into the dining room. They sat at same massive table where they'd sat a few nights ago, after she'd been attacked.

Ella came in with a pot of coffee just as Deputy Buford Watts and Guerrant came inside.

Buford didn't look the least bit surprised to see Reilly. "Delancey," he said resignedly. "First on the scene again?"

Reilly didn't bother to answer him. "Did you put out a BOLO for an armed man on foot running from this area?"

"Sure did. We'll see if anything comes of it." Buford turned to Christy. "Ms. Moser. Oh, I'm sorry. *Doctor* Moser. Have you thought about when you might want to be heading back to—" Buford looked at his notepad "—Boston?"

"Buford—" Reilly said warningly.

The deputy shrugged without taking his eyes off Christy.

"I'm not saying—I'm just saying. If I were attacked twice in one week, I might think about heading home."

CHRISTY WAS EXHAUSTED and shivering with fatigue by the time Deputy Watts got through questioning her and Reilly. His men had crawled all over her room, taking pictures, measuring the height of the broken windowpane and the height of the bullet hole in the wall and digging the slug out to preserve as evidence.

She watched dully as the deputy and his men left.

"Christy?"

It was Ella Bardin. "Christy, I really hate to say anything, but—"

"Please, Ella." Christy held up her hand. "You don't have to. I'll go to a hotel. I'm so sorry that I've put you and your husband in danger. And I'll certainly pay for the damage to the room."

"No, no," Ella protested. "I just might have to make up a tall tale, like maybe Jefferson Davis stayed here and somebody took a shot at him." She laughed.

Christy forced a smile. "Maybe that would work," she said. "Thank you so much for the coffee. Can I help you clean up?"

"Absolutely not. You just go ahead and get your stuff together."

Christy sighed. She'd hoped Ella would protest. That she'd insist that Christy could wait until morning to leave, but no such luck. Still, she certainly couldn't blame the woman. An assault and a shooting in the same week was never good for business or for peace of mind.

Reilly came in just as Christy pushed herself to her feet. "Get your stuff together?" He'd echoed Ella's words.

She nodded. "I'm going to get a hotel. I can't subject Ella and Guerrant to more violence."

"Well, you're not going to a hotel. You're coming with me."

Christy saw Ella pause on her way to the kitchen with the coffeepot. She turned around, obviously eavesdropping.

"Could we discuss this in my room?" Christy asked stiffly.

Reilly glanced toward Ella. "Okay, sure," he said, then leaned in close to her ear. "Although there's nothing to discuss."

She turned on her heel and headed through the door into her room. She waited for Reilly to enter, then closed the door behind him.

"I can't go to your apartment," she said. "I'll get a hotel room."

"The hell you will. There's somebody out there after you. If he can get to you here, he can get to you in a hotel. No. You're coming to my apartment."

"And why can't he get to me at your apartment?"

"Besides the fact that there's a security guard on duty 24/7? And it's on the eighth floor? Because *I'll* be there."

"A security guard?" she echoed. He lived in a secure apartment building? "No." She shook her head. "I can't."

"I don't see why not. Get packed."

"Because—" She stopped. She couldn't tell him why she didn't want to stay with him. She wasn't sure she could explain it to herself. She'd like to think it was because he was too overprotective, too bossy.

But that wasn't it. Or maybe it wasn't so much his protectiveness as her reaction to it. She'd always been independent. She liked living alone, making her own decisions, being in charge of her own life.

But as much as she tried to tell herself that Reilly's concern, his larger-than-life presence and his insistence on protecting her were annoying and unnecessary, she couldn't deny how good it felt to have someone concerned about her safety. She could get used to having a knight in shining armor around. And that was going to make it really hard to go back to her solitary, independent life. A life without Reilly Delancey in it.

"Christy? Are you sure you're all right?"

"What?" She realized she'd been staring at him. "Yes, of course. I can go to a hotel," she said unconvincingly, doing her best to look anywhere except at him.

"Get your stuff together." He didn't even bother arguing. "I'm going to check with Buford before he leaves, make sure he's got CSI collecting trace from inside and out."

Christy quickly packed her suitcase, checked around the room to make sure she hadn't forgotten anything and pulled her bag into the living room. She set the key in a dish on the coffee table and sat down to scribble a note on a sheet of Ella's Victorian writing paper.

Reilly came back inside. "Ready?" he asked as he grabbed her suitcase.

She picked up the key and slid the note beneath it. "Yes," she said.

"What's that?" he asked.

"Just a note to Ella to let her know how sorry I am for putting her in danger."

As they headed out to his car, she said, "I'll drive my rental car."

"No," Reilly responded flatly.

"I can't leave it sitting here in Ella's parking lot."

"It's been sitting here this long. It can stay for a few more days."

"But won't it make the…make him think I'm still here?"

Reilly looked at her thoughtfully. "Right. It could put Ella and Guerrant in more danger. I'll call the rental company and tell them to come pick it up. I'll pay any additional fees involved."

"That's ridiculous and unnecessary. I can drive." She dug in her purse for the keys.

"Yeah. That's the problem." With a movement so quick she had no time to react, Reilly grabbed the car keys from her hand. "You can drive, but you're not going to. I have no intention of letting you out of my sight. Now get in the car."

Christy's ears burned, she was so angry. "You're bossy and rude. This is tantamount to kidnapping."

Reilly's eyebrows shot up and he grinned. "Tantamount?"

Christy blew out her breath in a huff. "Bully," she muttered as she got into the car and slammed the passenger door.

CHRISTY HAD BEEN SURPRISED to say the least the first time she'd seen Reilly's condo. The view of Lake Pontchartrain alone had to be worth at least six figures. She'd guessed he'd paid at least a quarter million for it. In Boston, it would have been worth four times that. Although she doubted there were any condos this large in Boston.

Now as he led her down the hall to the guest suite, which was opposite the master suite, she revised her estimate of the condo's cost upward. The place had to be twenty-five hundred square feet, and the guest bath included a spa tub, a separate shower and one entire wall made of glass bricks.

Her amazement must have shown on her face, because he shrugged. "It came with the place," he said, repeating what he'd said the day before about the professional kitchen.

She just shook her head.

Giving her a narrow look, Reilly backed toward the door. "I'll let you—freshen up. If you need anything—"

Christy looked around. "I'm pretty sure there's nothing I could possibly think of that's not already here," she said.

Reilly nodded. "I don't suppose it would make a difference if I told you my cousin Cara Lynn furnished and decorated for me? I asked her to get whatever she thought I needed. Apparently she thought it would be funny to outfit the guest suite like some kind of luxury spa hotel or something."

She met his gaze, then glanced around the suite. There was a basket filled with bottles of water on a library table, alongside an exquisite silk arrangement in a bowl that probably cost more than the refrigerator in her apartment. A plasma TV was mounted above the marble fireplace opposite the bed.

The marble of the hearth extended to the right to form the entrance into the bath and dressing area, where Christy could see sparkling mirrors and shiny chrome fixtures.

"Apparently," she said. When her gaze met his again, he looked sheepish.

"Okay, then," he said. "If you need anything, pick up the phone. It'll buzz in my room and in the living room."

Christy uttered a short laugh. "Okay," she said.

Reilly's gaze faltered as he backed out the door and closed it behind him.

Christy frowned. Suddenly, he'd seemed ill at ease. Was it something she'd said? Maybe she'd embarrassed him about the opulence of the guest suite.

He'd said his cousin had decorated and furnished his apartment. She must have thought he'd have lots of guests. Had his cousin been thinking of female guests? But if so, why would she have thought the females would be staying in the guest suite, rather than in the master suite with Reilly?

Christy stepped past the marble fireplace and entered the bath. Her glimpse of chrome and mirrors and marble had been the tip of the iceberg. The bath was as large as her bedroom in Boston. The shower enclosure was clear glass. The spa tub was gigantic, with an unopened basket of bath accessories sitting on the wide tile ledge around it. The toilet was behind a half wall, and beside it was a bidet.

A bidet.

Christy chuckled softly. She'd love to meet his cousin. She was sure she'd like her. The first thing she'd do would be to thank her for giving Christy the first laugh she'd had in a long time. Then she'd thank her for the spa tub.

Her smile faded. All this opulence didn't fit with the Reilly Delancey she knew. Of course, all she knew was what he'd allowed her to see.

She sighed. She wasn't going to solve the dilemma of who Reilly was tonight.

She eyed the spa tub longingly. Maybe she could relax in the tub for a while. Maybe hot water and some fragrant bath salts would wash away the fear and tension and grime of the evening.

She quickly set her suitcase on the antique luggage rack in the dressing area and dug out fresh underwear and pajamas and her favorite gardenia-scented bath salts, then went into the bathroom and closed the door. A brand-new, snow-white bathrobe hung behind the door.

"Wow, all the amenities for Reilly's *guests*," she murmured. As she reached to turn on the hot water in the tub, she heard an unfamiliar chiming sound. She stopped. Was it a clock? A phone?

Phone. Her heart pounded. It was Autumn's phone.

Christy hurried over to her purse and upended it onto the bed. Where was that phone? It rang again. *There.*

She grabbed it with shaky hands. Who could be calling this number? Laurie? D.B.? Autumn's killer?

Finally, Christy got the phone turned around in her hand and was able to see the display. It was Laurie. She answered.

"Is this Christy?"

"Yes. Yes it is. Laurie?"

"I'm sorry to be calling so late—"

"It's not a problem. What is it, Laurie? Did you remember something?"

"Maybe. Did you say one of the names in her phone was Glo? G-L-O?"

"That's right."

"I think that might be a girl who went to high school with us. Her name was Gloria Soames. I didn't know her very well. She was really into Goth. You know, black clothes, black fingernails and lipstick. All that stuff. She dropped out before senior year."

Christy searched through the spilled contents of her purse, looking for a pen. She glanced at the bedside table. Of course there was a fancy, Victorian desk set complete with pen and notepaper. She grabbed the pen, holding it gingerly in her right hand—the one with the cast.

"Gloria Soames. Can you spell that?"

"I think it's S-O-A-M-E-S."

Christy wrote quickly. "What else do you know about her? Parents? Brothers and sisters? Where she lived?"

"She had a brother. He was older than us. His name was Jason or Jackson or something like that. Christy…" Laurie's voice faded. She knew something else. Something she didn't want to tell.

"Laurie? What is it?"

"You need to know. Glo was into drugs. Bad drugs—you know, needles and all that. And—" Laurie paused and Christy could hear her shaky breathing.

"And what?" Christy held her breath, afraid of what Laurie was about to tell her, but certain she knew what it was.

"Everybody talked about Glo. They all said she'd do anything to get money. Anything, you know?"

"I know," Christy said, rubbing her temples.

"I know that's not much, but—"

"Laurie, do you have a yearbook?"

"Um, sure. Somewhere."

"Can you look at it? See if you can find Glo and her brother, or the boy who played soccer. Was it Danny?"

"I guess so. Sure."

"Could you do it now? While we're on the phone?"

Laurie sighed. "I'm not sure where the book is."

Christy waited without speaking, hoping to guilt Laurie into finding it. She heard rustling sounds on the other end of the phone.

After a few long moments, and some huffing and puffing, Laurie said, "Here it is." She sneezed. "No, that's our senior year."

Another minute. "Okay. This is junior year."

"I can't tell you how much I appreciate this," Christy said.

"I had her name right. It's Gloria Soames. She was in our class. And here's Danny. His name is Danny Leader. I didn't think his last name began with a B. Now—" Laurie sneezed again. "Let me look at the seniors. Glo's brother was a year ahead of her—"

As she wrote down the names Laurie had given her, Christy could hear her turning pages.

"Okay. Gloria's brother's name is Jasper. Jasper Soames. He had tattoos and pierced ears even in high school."

Jasper Soames, Christy wrote. "Is there anyone else you can think of that she hung out with?"

"Not that I know of. I need to go. I have to pick up Aynsley at day care."

"Okay. Thank you so much, Laurie. I hope if you think of anything else, you'll call me and tell me. But let me give you my cell phone number. I don't know how long I can keep this phone." And she wanted the line open in case D.B. called.

Laurie took down her phone number and promised to call back if she thought of anything else.

Christy hung up. She folded the piece of stationery with the names on it and slid it into the bill pocket of her wallet. Tomorrow she was going to have to figure out how to find Gloria—Glo.

But tonight—

She went back into the bathroom and turned on the hot water, then began to undress. As the bathroom filled with steam and the scent of gardenias, her mind drifted back to Reilly and his cousin's superb taste in guest suites. She could get used to this kind of luxury.

That thought started a faint warning bell chiming in her mind. The more she considered Reilly's story about his cousin buying all his furniture and accessories for him, the more it unraveled.

Yes, it was plausible that he'd rented the place and then realized he didn't know anything about decorating. But for his cousin to have gone to all this trouble—all this detail and expense—was a little odd.

Yet wouldn't it be even more odd if Reilly had done all this himself? And therein lay the problem. This guest suite was designed and outfitted to wrap a woman in sensuous luxury. But what woman?

Had his cousin really done all this as a joke? Or was he just using her as an excuse? What if he'd bought and furnished this apartment with a woman—his wife or his fiancée?

What if he'd outfitted himself an ultimate bachelor pad?

Of course, it didn't matter to her. Or it shouldn't anyway.

She knew nothing about Reilly Delancey. For all she knew he had a veritable parade of women through here, each of whom doused herself with expensive bath salts and wrapped herself in decadently fluffy bathrobes.

Be careful, she warned herself. Reilly seemed like an unpretentious, down-to-earth kind of guy. But looking at his condo and trying to imagine the kind of money he'd spent on it and its furnishings, Christy wondered which was the real Reilly Delancey—the protective, concerned lawman or the wealthy, self-indulgent Delancey heir?

Chapter Nine

Reilly got almost no sleep. Images of what could have happened to Christy kept swirling in his head.

Christy standing in front of the dresser, the bullet impacting her in the side and knocking her to the floor, her lifeblood seeping into the hardwood boards.

The faceless killer taking aim, squeezing the trigger then escaping through the vacant lot, leaving telltale DNA in the form of droplets of blood on the sharp twigs and briars.

He must have drifted off a few times because occasionally those horrific nightmares morphed into sensual dreams.

Christy sinking into a steaming tub of water, bath oils and perfumes glistening on her skin, her black hair pinned up but falling.

Him holding a soft white towel out for her as she rose from the steam, rivulets of glistening water running down between her breasts, down to her waist and hips, her belly and farther.

Finally, around five o'clock, he got up and took a shower—first cold because he had to, then hot. He threw on a pair of comfortable jeans and made a pot of coffee.

With mug in hand, he spread Autumn Moser's case file out on his dining room table and started reading, occasionally pausing to input a note or an impression into his mini-notebook computer.

He'd made it almost through the case file and was on page eleven of his notes when he heard the door to the guest suite open.

He looked up as Christy walked into the living room and squinted at the glass wall, where the sun was just beginning to light the sky. She had on pink satin pajamas that matched the cast on her wrist and left her arms and her slender ankles bare.

Pink pajamas. He smiled. That was interesting. He didn't think she'd had time to go shopping, so the pajamas must have been packed in her suitcase. And that meant, despite her grousing about the cast, she did in fact like pink. What else was she hiding under her crisply tailored clothes?

He let his gaze slide over her body. The tips of her breasts were clearly outlined by the slinky material, and the way it draped left little doubt as to how shapely her slender body was. He felt like a voyeur. She obviously had no idea he was sitting there.

He held his breath and didn't move as she turned from the window toward the kitchen. It was rude not to announce himself, but he wanted to watch her a little longer. It was the first time he'd had a chance to really study her at leisure. One or both of them had always been busy when they'd been together before.

Her hair was glossy and black. It caught and absorbed the dim early morning light like velvet, and cast enticing shadows along the elegant curve of her neck and shoulders.

He clenched his jaw against the heat that rose in his groin at the sheer womanliness of her.

She started as if he'd made a sound and her gaze darted to the dining table where he sat.

"Oh," she said. "I didn't know you were up." Her hand fluttered to her chest as if to try and shield her breasts from his eyes.

"Morning," he responded. "I was beginning to think you were sleepwalking."

She uttered a little sound, like a soft *harrumph*. "I don't sleepwalk." Her hand still hovered over her breasts, but finally she reached up and pushed her hair back. "Do I smell coffee?"

Apparently modesty lost out to the need for caffeine.

"Yep. It's been there a while. Want me to make fresh?"

"No. It'll do."

"The mugs and sugar are there, next to the pot. Cream's in the refrigerator. What are you doing up?"

She shook her head as she poured coffee and sweetened it. "I couldn't sleep. I kept dreaming about gunshots."

"Yeah, me too," he said wryly. "I've been going over your sister's case file."

Christy came over to the table and sat down beside him. "Autumn's case file?" she echoed. "How long have you had that? Why didn't you tell me?"

"I just got it day before yesterday. This is the first chance I've gotten to look at it. Plus, we've been a little busy."

She acknowledged the truth of his statement with a nod. "So what have you found out?"

"Nothing I didn't already know from Ryker's notes. Basically, it looks like the detective who caught the case wrote it off as a mugging without really looking into it." He paused. "I'm sorry."

She waved a hand. "I already knew that. What I don't understand is why." She took a breath. "I mean, she was shot point-blank in the chest, three times. How could anyone think a mugger would do that? Even if the detective wrote it up that way, aren't those reports reviewed by someone?"

Reilly shrugged. "It was right after Katrina. The police were overworked and exhausted. I know it won't make you feel better, but your sister's case was probably not the only one that got swept under the rug."

"You're right. That doesn't make me feel better at all. It makes me angry. Why didn't the police have more help? Katrina was a national—an international disaster."

"Hey." He held up his hands. "You're preaching to the choir here. Even now, there are still dozens of people missing, dozens of unidentified bodies. Scores of lives ruined." He stopped, clenching his jaw. "Sorry. I'll put my soapbox away."

She acknowledged his frustration and his apology with a small nod. "What about that detective?" she asked, moving the conversation back to her agenda. "Who is he? Can anything be done about him?"

"Name's Samhurst. I doubt it. But what we can do is look further into the case. It's a long shot, but maybe we can find a witness, or a friend of your sister's, who can give us a clue as to what happened."

Christy wrapped both hands around her mug and looked into its depths for a few seconds.

Reilly watched her. Her body language told him she was unsure about something. Or trying to decide what to do about something. But what? He thought about his last words. *A friend of your sister's.* Did she know someone? If so, why not tell him?

He stayed quiet while she finished her internal debate.

Finally she took a deep swallow of coffee. "Mmm, chicory coffee?" she asked.

Disappointment slid through him. Her evasive comment convinced him that she had information she wasn't telling him.

He took a long breath. "Yep. Maybe later I'll boil some milk and make us a café au lait." He made a point of glancing at his notes. "Nobody ever asked you or your dad about Autumn's friends?"

"They did, but I couldn't really help them. I don't think Dad did either. I was interviewed by a very fat detective—if you could call it an interview. I don't think it lasted twenty minutes. I told him I'd been on the phone with Autumn when she was shot, but all he did was have me write out a statement. His comment was that they didn't find her—" Christy stopped, and Reilly noticed that her fingers tightened around the mug. "—her phone," she finished.

Alarm bells rang in his head. *Autumn's phone.*

"What is it?" he asked. "Did you remember something?"

"No," she said, so quickly that he was sure she had. "Nothing. It's just—hard to remember how unconcerned he was. I'll bet he never even looked at my statement."

Reilly let his gaze slide over her body. The whitened tips of her fingers, her bent head and the stiffness in her shoulders indicated a high level of stress. Stress because she was lying? Or stress due to the events of the last two days? Maybe combined with the pain of reliving her sister's murder?

Naturally she was traumatized by her two near misses and her father's heart attack, but he didn't think that was all that was bothering her.

He'd been around her enough to read her pretty well. He'd bet his condo that she was hiding something from him.

He'd been a hostage negotiator long enough to know her personality type too. If he tried to bully her into telling him what was on her mind, she'd clam up. He had to co-opt her. He'd continue to do what he'd been doing, offering himself as a confidant, proving to her that she could trust him.

"So you didn't know any of her friends?"

She shook her head. "Not after she got out of high school. I told the detective about her best friend in school—Laurie

Kestler. But I can guarantee you that Laurie didn't know any drug users."

"How? How are you sure? I mean—she was a friend of Autumn's."

"They'd been friends since grade school. I'm not sure how much they saw each other after Autumn got deep into drugs. But I've known Laurie for years. Trust me, she's not the type."

"Not the type? Is that your professional opinion? Because it's not always that easy to tell, you know. Before you knew that Autumn was into drugs, wouldn't you have said that she wasn't the type?"

Christy set the mug down and looked at him, her face reflecting doubt. A tiny wrinkle appeared between her brows. "I don't know."

He stared at her. She'd lied to him about so many things, but now she was telling the truth. He had to admire her honesty, in this instance at least. Many families of drug users responded automatically to that question. *Of course. I could never have believed that my daughter/son/sister/brother would turn to drugs.*

"And yet you're sure Laurie wasn't? Why?"

Christy averted her gaze again. If he was reading her right, and he was pretty darn sure he was, she'd talked to Laurie. Recently. Maybe today.

"When was the last time you talked to Laurie? Was she at Autumn's funeral?"

Christy looked up. "Yes, she came to the funeral. But I didn't talk to her other than the usual stuff people say at funerals."

Pretty smooth. He gave his head a mental shake. He'd made the mistake of asking two questions at once, and Christy had parried him quite nicely. She hadn't answered his first question. She'd gone straight to the second.

He made a mental note to find Laurie. "Do you know how to get in touch with her? What did you say her last name is? Kestler?"

Again, Christy didn't answer him directly. "When Autumn was killed, Laurie was in school in Florida. I'm not sure where. She's—she's probably married by now."

"What about her parents?"

Christy picked up her mug and stood. "Want some more coffee?"

He shook his head.

She rounded the kitchen island and poured herself another mug of coffee. The teaspoon chimed against the mug as she stirred in sugar. Her shoulders were stiff, her back ramrod straight.

"Christy? Laurie's parents?"

"I'm not sure. I didn't know them. I'll check the phone book." She turned around. "What are you doing today?"

"First I'm going by the sheriff's office to check with Watts about that bullet we dug out of the wall. I'm hoping we can get a match. I'm betting that gun has been involved in a violent crime somewhere along the way."

Christy took a sip of coffee. "Can you take me to the hospital today? If not, I'll be glad to rent another car."

Reilly opened his mouth, but one look at her face and he decided she was baiting him. He didn't feel like biting. "Sure. No problem. How soon can you be ready?"

"Half hour."

"Good. You didn't answer my question. Autumn's friend Laurie. Did you say her last name was Kestler?"

"Oh, sorry. Yes. K-E-S-T-L-E-R. But—" She paused. "But it seems to me like they were retiring and moving away— maybe to Florida. That's where Laurie went to school."

"Where in Florida?"

Christy shrugged without looking at him. "I have no idea.

I'm going to take my coffee back to the bedroom and get dressed."

Reilly nodded, tamping down his irritation. Once she'd closed the door to the guest suite, he doubled his fist and slammed it down on the table.

"Damn it, Christy," he muttered. "What are you doing? Why do you keep lying to me?"

AFTER REILLY TOOK CHRISTY to the hospital, he headed over to see if Buford Watts was on duty. Since it was Saturday morning, he doubted that Watts had heard anything back from the lab about the bullet they'd dug out of the wall at the Oak Grove Inn. But he wanted to check.

He found Buford painfully typing up his report using two fingers. "Deputy Watts. Working the weekend?"

Buford sent him a dirty look. "Wouldn't have to if people didn't get shot at on Friday night. What the hell are you doing here?"

"What'd you get on that bullet?"

"I figured you'd be around this morning wanting to know that. Nothing here. I've got someone checking the NOPD database just in case."

"Good. I was going to ask if you'd do that."

Buford stood and picked up his coffee cup. He gestured with it toward the coffeepot that sat on a table next to a water cooler. Reilly shook his head but followed Buford, who poured himself a cup of the strong, vile-smelling stuff.

"What is it with you and that serial killer's daughter?"

Reilly grabbed a paper cup and filled it with water and downed it. "She needs to know what happened to her sister. Needs to understand how her sister's death affected her father."

Buford snorted. "It turned him into a serial killer, that's how it affected him."

Reilly nodded reluctantly. "That's what you and I see. But what Christy sees is that her sister is dead and her father might as well be. You know he had a heart attack, right? She feels like she's lost her whole family. She needs answers and I intend to find them for her."

"So you fancy yourself some kind of Don Quixote?"

Reilly raised an eyebrow at the detective. "Don Quixote?"

"Yeah, what? You didn't know I could read?"

"I figured you could read. But I didn't picture you as a romantic."

Buford eyed him narrowly. "I'm pretty sure I'm not the romantic here."

"Give me a call as soon as you hear something about that bullet, will you?"

"Deputy Watts," a rookie deputy called out, waving a sheet of paper. "This fax just came in for you."

Buford took a gulp of coffee. "Well, bring it over here, kid."

The young man brought him the sheet of paper and Reilly moved closer to read over Buford's shoulder.

"It's about the bullet," Reilly said, unable to contain his excitement.

"Yeah," Buford drawled, taking his time reading the fax. "Looks like the bullet we took out of the wall of your girlfriend's room matches the bullets recovered from the body of a mugging victim, Autumn Moser—" Buford's voice stopped. He raised his gaze to Reilly's.

"What?" Reilly grabbed the sheet of paper. Had Watts said what Reilly thought he had?

"Hey!" Buford yelled. "Gimme that!"

"Autumn Moser! That's Christy's sister. This means whoever shot at Christy last night used the same gun that was used to kill her sister. I'll be damned! Whoever he was, he kept the gun." Reilly's chest was burning with excitement. Was it really going to be this easy?

Now, if they could just get a lead on who had been outside the Oak Grove Inn last night, shooting at Christy, maybe they'd have Autumn Moser's killer. "You've got to love stupid criminals."

"Delancey, give me that fax," Buford said. "I'm warning you."

"Can I get a copy of it?"

Buford shot him a warning look. "When it's logged into evidence and made a part of the record of the shooting last night, I'll get you a copy."

Reilly opened his mouth.

"And not one second before," Buford snapped. "You know the procedures."

"Yeah, I do. But Buford—that'll be Monday. You could just run me a copy, since it's the weekend. This could be the break I've been looking for. If I can find that gun, I'll have Autumn Moser's killer."

"This isn't your case, Delancey. I'll get you the information as soon as I get it."

"And anything else you find out about that bullet, as soon as possible." Reilly thought about Detective Samhurst's report from Autumn Moser's case file. "Wait a minute. There's a partial fingerprint on one of the shell casings they found near Autumn Moser's body. I've got the file. I'll fax a copy to you as soon as I get home."

As Reilly headed out, he heard Buford's voice behind him. "Watch out for those windmills, Quixote."

CHRISTY SAT IN A straight-backed chair in her father's cubicle in the cardiac care unit. He was asleep. The nurse had explained that he was being given morphine to keep him sedated because of the lidocaine, which they were giving him to maintain his heart rate. Lidocaine caused hallucinations in some patients, and the attending physician wanted Mr. Moser to be as quiet as possible so as not to overtax his heart. He was already on oxygen.

Any further stress, the nurse had said, and they'd have to put him on a ventilator.

Christy knew from her own medical training that the prognosis for her dad wasn't good.

The cardiologist had discussed with her the amount of damage the myocardial infarction had done to his heart muscle. She knew, unless a miracle occurred, that it was only a matter of time before she'd have to make the decision whether or not to put him on a ventilator to breathe for him. She agreed with the cardiologist that the chances of him surviving the amount of damage to his heart were extremely slim.

The nurse stuck her head around the curtain. "Dr. Moser, I'm afraid morning visiting hours are over. I could let you stay about five more minutes, but—"

"No, that's fine. I know you have rounds. I'll get out of your way." She stood and kissed her dad on the forehead then stepped out of the room.

"I have an appointment," she told the nurse. "I won't make it back here in time for the noon visitation, I know. If I can't get back before the afternoon visitation is over, can I check with you about seeing him for a few minutes once I do make it back?"

"I go off duty at four. But I'll let the evening nurse know," the nurse said, smiling at her. "Meanwhile, we'll take good care of him."

Christy walked down the hall past the CCU waiting room and on to the elevators. She glanced at her watch. Reilly had asked her if she'd be okay until he got back at around four-thirty. She'd said that was fine. She'd be there for three visitation times: ten o'clock, noon and four o'clock.

At the time, she'd been sincere. But while she was waiting for the slow hands of the clock to move around to ten o'clock, she'd dialed the number listed for Glo on Autumn's SIM card. A man had answered.

"Can I speak to Glo?" she'd asked.

After a pause, the man had asked, "Who is this?"

"A friend," she'd mumbled.

"Yeah? Well, if you were a friend, you'd know Glo ain't here. Why don't you try her deadbeat brother, Jazzy?"

Christy had hung up, then paged through the list of contacts until she'd come to the number listed for *Jazzy*. She'd pressed the call button.

A rusty voice had answered. Christy hadn't been able to tell if it was a man or a woman. She'd pitched her own voice low and gravelly. "Glo?"

"Yeah?"

Surprised that she'd actually reached the girl, she'd cleared her throat. "Glo," she'd said in a more normal voice. "My name's Christy. I'm Autumn Moser's sister."

"Wha—? Who?"

"Glo. I need to talk to you. You were Autumn's friend, right?"

"Autumn? She's dead." The words had been halting and a bit slurred.

"I know. Where are you? I need to ask you something. And—" Christy had paused, wondering if what she was about to do was illegal. She was a physician, and it sounded like Glo was an addict. There were laws about writing prescriptions for known addicts. But did those laws extend to providing them with the money to buy drugs themselves?

Even if she was skirting the law, it was the best chance she'd gotten yet to find out who Autumn had been with on the day she died. She'd decided it was worth any possible risk.

"Glo, Autumn wanted you to have something. Can I bring it to you?"

"Me? What?" The voice had perked up slightly at Christy's words.

"Well, it's—it's money, actually."

Christy's ruse had worked. Glo's tone had changed immediately, once she heard the word *money*. She had given Christy an address in a rough section of Mandeville.

Exiting the elevator on the first floor of the hospital, Christy walked quickly out to the curb and flagged a taxi. When she told the driver where she wanted to go, he stared at her.

"Salvation Road? No way. I don't go down there."

She held up a hundred-dollar bill. "There's another one for you if you'll take me there and wait for me."

The driver took the hundred, then met her gaze in the rearview mirror. "Lady, you sure you know what you're doing?"

Christy didn't answer him, she just waved a second bill.

The driver flipped the meter. "Extra C-note or no, I ain't sticking around if there's any trouble."

Christy swallowed hard, but nodded. All she could do was hope there wouldn't be a reason for him to leave.

It took over twenty minutes to get to Salvation Road. He stopped at a row of shotgun houses that were badly in need of repair. A few were nothing but roofless shells. The street looked as if it had been devastated by a hurricane last week rather than five years before.

Christy got out of the taxi. "Please don't leave me," she said to the driver. "Honk or something if you can't wait any longer and I'll come out. I promise. This shouldn't take more than a couple of minutes anyway."

The driver nodded once. She didn't believe for a second that he'd honk to warn her before he got the hell out of there. She had to hurry.

Chapter Ten

She knocked on the cracked and peeling door. After about fifteen seconds, when no one appeared, she knocked again.

The woman who answered the door was definitely impaired by something. When she opened the door a crack to peer out, Christy saw how pale and thin she was. Her hair was unwashed and stringy, and the T-shirt she wore had stains on it that Christy didn't even want to speculate about. Dear God, had Autumn lived like this?

"Are you Glo?" she asked.

"Who wants to know?" the woman rasped.

"I'm Christy Moser."

Glo wiped her red nose with the back of her hand as she squinted against the bright afternoon sunlight. "What happened to you?" she asked.

"I was attacked." She waved a hand. "That's not why I'm here."

"Yeah," the girl muttered. "You got something for me?"

Christy took a deep breath and said more firmly, "Yes, as soon as you answer a few questions."

Glo frowned and glanced behind her, then nodded. "I thought it was a gift, from Autumn."

Christy shrugged. "I made that up."

Glo grimaced. "Well, you better not stand out there."

Christy glanced back at the taxi. The driver was scowling, but at least he was still there.

This is probably a big mistake, she thought as she stepped inside. The dark, cramped living room was strewn with foam containers, discarded clothes and beer cans. Ashtrays overflowed with cigarette butts. The air stunk of all of that and more—much of it rank and distressingly identifiable.

Glo stood with her back against the closed front door. "What do you want to know?" she asked hoarsely.

"You knew my sister, Autumn."

"Yeah."

Christy sighed. This wasn't going to be easy. "I need to know who she was seeing. Who she was with the day she died."

Glo shook her head. "I ain't got no idea," she muttered, crossing her thin arms across her chest.

"Glo, please. You were in school with her. You must know something."

"What's going on?" Glo asked. "Autumn's been dead for a long time."

Christy nodded miserably. "Five years. I didn't take care of her when she was alive. But I want to find out who killed her."

The girl ducked her head. "I heard it was a mugging."

Christy lay her hand on the girl's thin arm. "You know it wasn't. Come on, Glo. Give me something."

Glo looked beyond her. Christy forced herself not to turn and follow the girl's gaze. There was someone else in the house. Someone Glo was afraid of.

"I've got money—just for you—but I need a name. Who was Autumn seeing? The day she died was her birthday. She went out with someone. Who was it?"

Glo grimaced and Christy saw her blackened teeth. "I swear, I don't know who she was with that night, but she—"

Glo's arms tightened and her knuckles went white. "She used to get drugs from a guy named Kramer." Glo looked up at Christy. "She'd trade—stuff—for drugs."

Stuff. Christy winced. She knew what Glo was saying, although she wished she didn't. "Kramer," she repeated. "What's his first name?"

Glo shrugged, not looking at her.

"Come on, Glo. He sells drugs. I know you know him. Tell me his name."

"Buddy."

"What?"

"His name. All I know is Buddy."

"Do you know where I can find him?"

"I can't—look, uh—Christy. I need my money." Glo's gaze shifted behind Christy again. "Now."

Christy held up a folded stack of twenties. "This is a hundred dollars. You've got my phone number in your phone. If you remember something else, I'll give you more."

Glo reached for the money. Christy took a step backward. "Where can I find Buddy Kramer?"

Swallowing visibly, Glo eyed the money. "He works downtown, out of an abandoned hotel called the Winsor."

Christy pressed the twenties into Glo's outstretched hand. "Remember what I said," she muttered. "If you think of anything else—"

"What the hell? Glo!" A sharp male voice cracked the air like thunder.

Christy jumped and whirled.

"Jazzy, I wasn't—"

"Shut up! Who the hell are you?" The man, a medium-height scarecrow in a torn T-shirt and filthy jeans, got in Christy's face. His breath was as rank as the room, smelling of stale cigarettes, sour beer and onions.

She recoiled, moving toward the door.

"I said—" He lifted his hand in a threatening gesture.

"Jazzy!" Glo snapped with more energy than Christy had seen from her. "She just had some questions about a friend of hers. A girl I used to hang out with."

Jazzy whirled toward Glo. "Oh, yeah?" He shot a suspicious look back at Christy. "You don't look like you got any friends that would hang out with my sister. But I'm sure I'd know him—or her. Who is it?"

"It doesn't matter," Christy said with more bravado than she felt. "She's dead now. I was trying to find her—her boyfriend. He has some—personal stuff that I want back."

Jazzy sized her up with a narrowed gaze. "I'll bet Glo could help you for a price, couldn't you, Glo?" He turned to glare at the girl.

Christy held her breath as Glo answered. It was obvious that Glo didn't want Jazzy to know she'd given her money. "I couldn't tell her anything, Jaz." Glo's fist, which held the rolled-up twenties Christy had given her, tightened.

"Oh, yeah?" Jazzy scrutinized Glo then turned back to Christy. "Ask me, gorgeous," he said. "I'll tell you something. Just how much money we talking anyhow?"

"Who said anything about money?" Christy responded. "I was just trying to find my friend."

"Oh, yeah?" Jazzy's vocabulary was obviously limited. He stepped closer, grinning at her. He was a couple of inches shorter than she was in her heels.

She straightened and lifted her chin, glaring down at him. "That's right. I have to go now." She turned toward the door, but Jazzy grabbed her arm.

"Ow!" She winced and pulled against his grip.

"Hang on a minute, gorgeous. I didn't say you could leave."

"Let me go," Christy demanded, pulling against Jazzy's rock-hard grip. "Are you threatening me?"

Out of the corner of her eye, Christy saw Glo stuff the twenties into her tight jeans and advance on her brother. "Jaz. Stop that!" she shouted, doubling her fist and hitting him in the bicep. "Let go of her."

"Hey, bitch! What'd I tell you about hitting me." Christy was forgotten as Jazzy whirled on his sister, raising his arm, prepared to backhand her across the face.

"Get outta here!" Glo shrieked at her.

Christy hesitated for a fraction of a second, afraid for Glo. But it looked as if she and her brother had fought like this for a long time.

At that instant, Glo jerked back from Jazzy's threatening gesture and a small can of pepper spray appeared in her hand.

"What'd I tell you about hitting *me!*" she yelled.

Yes, it looked like Glo could handle Jazzy. Christy jerked the door open and ran. She saw the taxi driver looking past her at the open door of the ramshackle house. As she ran toward him he started the engine.

She jumped into the backseat. "Okay," she said breathlessly, pushing her hair back with a shaky hand. "Go! Get out of here."

The driver was still looking toward the house as he put the car into gear. Then he met her gaze in the rearview mirror. After a couple of seconds, he laughed. "You gotta be crazy," he said. Then he held up his hand. "Give me my C-note."

Christy's heart was beating so fast that she felt like she couldn't breathe. She squeezed her eyes shut and worked to get herself under control.

"Not yet. When you get me safely back to the hospital," she snapped, rubbing her arm.

NOT AN HOUR AFTER REILLY had faxed the partial print from Autumn Moser's file to Buford Watts's office, the deputy called him. He was on his way to the hospital to pick up Christy.

"We got a match on that print," Watts said.

"Already?" Reilly was surprised.

"Yeah. I went ahead and ran it, since I was going to be here all day anyhow."

"Well? Who is it?"

"Print belongs to a dealer who operates in downtown Mandeville, around the old Hotel Winsor." Reilly heard papers shuffling. "Name's Buddy Kramer."

"So Kramer's a known dealer?"

"Yep." Buford's reply was short and noncommittal.

Reilly knew what that meant. Somebody was using Kramer as a confidential informant. Otherwise he'd probably be in prison. "What now?"

Watts sighed. "I gotta pick him up for questioning."

Reilly thanked Watts for calling him and hung up, then called his brother.

Ryker answered the phone with a sleepy growl.

"Afternoon," Reilly said cheerfully. "What's up?"

Another growl.

Reilly figured he knew what Ryker was doing on a Saturday afternoon. "Sorry to interrupt you and your lovely fiancée, but I need some information."

Ryker grunted, muttered a curse and yawned. "Is this something to do with Moser's daughter?"

"It is. Are you familiar with a two-bit dealer named Buddy Kramer?"

"Kramer?" Ryker yawned again.

"Come on, old man. Think. This is important."

"Kramer. Okay. I think Charlie Phillips has a CI named Kramer. Why?"

"A partial print of Kramer's was in Autumn Moser's case

file, and last night Christy was shot at. The shell casing from the bullet has Kramer's print on it."

"Crap." Now Ryker's voice was sharp.

"Yeah," Reilly agreed.

"I didn't think that print in Autumn Moser's file had an ID attached to it."

"It didn't. Buford Watts matched the bullet in the system."

"It was the same gun?"

"Right."

"Charlie Phillips is a good detective. He wouldn't—"

"I believe you," Reilly said, "but it's going to be touchy. Christy found a bag of heroin in her sister's room that was marked by one of the crime scene analysts, Amber Madden."

"A marked bag?"

"Right. Do you see where this is going? I'm beginning to think Autumn's boyfriend was a cop."

"Son of a bitch!"

"Exactly." Reilly's reaction when the thought first popped into his head had been exactly the same.

"Kid, you need to be careful. You can't just go on a witch hunt. You could destroy a detective's career because they might have hooked up with some girl somewhere."

"*That's* what you think I'm doing?" Reilly said, ire rising at Ryker's assumption that he'd go off half-cocked.

"So what are you doing?"

"I'm trying to find out who killed Autumn Moser."

There was silence on the other end of the phone.

"What about Bill Crenshaw?" Ryker's friend.

"What about him?" Ryker's tone took on an edge.

"Does he have a CI?"

More silence.

"So he does. Do you know who it is?"

"No."

"Come on, old man. Help me out here. You work with Bill all the time. Are you telling me you don't know who his CI is?"

"Why do you think they call them *confidential?* They're not much use if everybody knows who they are."

"What about the other detectives? Who else uses them?"

"Hell, I don't know. Maybe half of the guys."

"Can you find out?"

Another pause. "I'll see."

Reilly took a deep breath. He needed to ask one more question. "Ryker? What about you?" Reilly was pretty sure what his brother's answer was, but he wanted to hear it.

"Nope. It always seemed a little sleazy to me. I have used information from them before though, when I work with a detective who uses them."

"Okay, thanks."

"You got any more questions?"

"Nope. I'm done for now. Tell Nicole I said hi."

"Reilly says hi," Ryker said in an aside.

"Hi to Reilly," he heard Nicole say.

"Listen, kid," Ryker said. "Be careful. If you suspect somebody on the job, be sure of your facts. You could ruin a good man's career—and your own."

REILLY KNEW SOMETHING was up with Christy as soon as he saw her. It wasn't so much how she acted or what she did, as what she didn't do. She didn't walk confidently through the hospital entrance doors, her head held high. She didn't tilt her head at that arrogant angle he was used to seeing, and she didn't mow down the men in her path with a look.

Something had happened in the hours since he'd left her here. He leaned over and opened the passenger door for her.

She got in without saying anything and busied herself with fastening her seat belt.

He pulled out onto the highway, heading toward his apartment. "How's your dad?" he asked.

"The same," she said shortly. "He's not getting any better."

"I'm sorry. Do you have other family anywhere? Someone I could call for you?"

She shook her head. "My mother had a sister who lived somewhere around St. Louis, but they weren't close and I don't even know her married name."

"Your aunt? You don't know your aunt's name?"

"That's right."

Reilly was stunned. "How can you not—?"

From the corner of his eye he saw her chin lift defiantly. He bit back that question and went down another path.

"What about your dad?"

"My dad?"

"His parents. His siblings."

"My grandparents are dead. Dad had two brothers, both of whom died in their fifties of heart disease. They had kids. We saw them a couple of times at holidays, but—" She waved a hand. "You know."

That's just it. He didn't know. His family had always been close. Sometimes—okay, a lot of the time—they didn't get along, but they were still close. He knew his first cousins as well as he knew his brothers. He couldn't imagine not knowing aunts and uncles or his cousins. He shrugged.

"What do the doctors say?"

"They're telling me that it could be a matter of days or weeks. It all depends on whether he has another heart attack. They're warning me that I need to start thinking about things. Like whether I want to put him on a ventilator."

Reilly waited, but Christy didn't say anything else.

"Do you?"

She shook her head as he drove into the private parking garage of his building. He parked and came around to open her car door for her. Both of them were silent as they went into the elevators and up to Reilly's apartment.

Once they were inside, he turned to her. "Christy? Do you know what you want to do? Do you know what your father wants?"

"He told me once that his dad lingered for weeks because he and his brothers let the doctors put a feeding tube in. He said he didn't want to be kept alive if it was time for him to go."

Reilly put his hand on her back in a comforting gesture. "You stayed there at the hospital all day. You must be exhausted."

She stepped away from him and rubbed her forehead. "I am tired. And I need to take a shower." She took another step backward, toward the guest room.

"Sure," he said. "Go ahead." He watched her as she walked to the guest room door and opened it. Her shoulders were slumped. Her hair didn't have that sheen of black velvet. And if he wasn't mistaken, there was a faint smell of cigarette smoke clinging to her.

As if she heard his thoughts, she turned at the door with a grimace. "Some guy kept sneaking cigarettes—in the waiting room bathroom, I think. I started to report him. He reeked of smoke. Stank up the entire waiting room. I'm sure I smell like smoke now."

Reilly didn't comment. He just watched her steadily as she lowered her gaze and went inside.

Once the door had closed behind her, he let out a frustrated breath. "You're lying," he whispered. She'd withdrawn when he said she'd been at the hospital all day and she'd gone to a lot of trouble to explain away cigarette smoke that for all she knew, he hadn't even noticed.

A righteous anger grew in his chest. Righteous, yes, but also concerned. She was worried about her dad, but not so much that it had kept her from sneaking off again. He didn't believe for a second that anyone had been sneaking cigarettes in the bathroom. She'd been somewhere with someone who'd smoked. A taxi driver? Or someone she'd arranged to meet? He paced back and forth in front of the guest room door.

"Damn it, Christy," he muttered. "Why won't you trust me? You're going to get yourself killed."

He stopped and clenched his fists. He ought to go in there right now and give her a piece of his mind, then put her in protective custody, assign a couple of deputies to watch her 24/7. Well, he could, if the department weren't so shorthanded right now.

A thought occurred to him. He didn't have to depend on an overtaxed police force. He could hire someone himself— maybe one of Dawson's specialists. His older brother's security firm employed women and men.

But he couldn't force Christy to accept what essentially amounted to imprisonment. So the security specialist would be no more effective at keeping up with her than Reilly himself was.

He stomped into the kitchen to get some water, his brain whirling. Where had she gone today? Her dad's house? No. She'd already found what she'd been looking for there.

Or had she? Whatever she'd hoped to find in Autumn's secret hiding place, it wasn't money or drugs. But there was nothing else there, she'd told him. Nothing but some coins and a ribbon.

That was a lie too. She'd definitely found something else— he was sure of it. She'd been acting suspiciously ever since then. Showing him the drugs and money and getting them into police hands hadn't made her less uneasy.

In fact, she seemed more nervous than ever.

Whatever she'd found, she had no intention of telling him about it. If he was going to protect her, he was going to have to force her to trust him somehow.

Force her. Yeah. That would work.

He looked at his watch. Nearly eight. She'd been in there almost an hour. She ought to be through with her shower by now. He strode back into the kitchen and opened the refrigerator. She probably hadn't eaten, and he was starving. There was some sliced ham that had been in there over a week. He inspected the neon-green sheen on some of the slices. Nope. He tossed it in the trash. Then he opened the freezer. A frozen pasta entree. A pizza. Ice cream.

He read the ingredients on the package. Mushrooms and shrimp in a Parmesan cream sauce with rigatoni. Sounded pretty good. He hadn't lied when he said he didn't cook, but he'd tried a few of these all-in-one-package meals. They weren't bad, and they were easy. Add water and cook on low heat. Even he could do that.

He did exactly what the package said, and within twenty minutes he had dinner ready. He took a domestic Sauv Blanc out of the wine cooler and opened it.

As he took another look at his watch, his phone rang. It was Ryker.

"Hey, old man," he said. "Did you finally decide to get out of bed?"

Ryker ignored him. "I talked to Bill."

"Yeah?" Had Ryker told his friend about Reilly's questions?

"I managed to bring up the topic of confidential informants. Bill said Kramer used to be Ted Dagewood's CI, but a few years ago Dagewood dropped him and picked up another guy. Bill wasn't sure of the new guy's name."

"Dagewood *dropped* Kramer? What does that even mean?"

"Don't know. According to Bill, Dagewood didn't like some of the things Kramer was doing."

"He said Dagewood dropped Kramer a few years ago? Like five maybe?"

"I know what you're thinking. That would have been around the time Autumn Moser was killed," Ryker said. "I don't know. Where are you going with this? Are you thinking Dagewood was involved with Christy's sister?" Ryker snorted. "I'd sooner suspect Phillips. Dagewood's so uptight. I can't see him doing anything that would jeopardize his career."

Reilly felt a chill run down his spine. That was almost exactly what Moser had said about Autumn's boyfriend. "Okay. Thanks. I appreciate the information."

"No problem. By the way, Mom called about the party. Are you going to bring your gorgeous doctor?"

Reilly winced. "I doubt it. She's not very happy with me right now. In fact, I'm not very happy with her. She's lying to me every time she opens her mouth."

"Well, think about it. Can you see Mom if we both ended up engaged?"

Reilly laughed. "Engaged? That's *you*, old man. Not me."

"Watch out. You'll find yourself in over your head before you realize it."

Reilly thanked his brother for the advice and hung up. He checked his watch, then headed back to the guest suite door. "Christy?" he called out, then rapped quietly. "Christy?"

She was probably soaking in the tub. He should just wait.

No, maybe he shouldn't wait. She'd been lying to him ever

since he'd known her. Damn her, she'd asked for his help. Now it seemed like she was doing her best to get away from him.

I thought you were your brother. Her words echoed in his head. It didn't matter. She'd asked. And whether she wanted to admit it or not, she did need him.

That thought triggered another one. One he didn't want to consider. Despite his irritation, even anger, at her lies, he couldn't deny that he was getting used to having her around. Worse, he liked it.

You'll find yourself in over your head before you realize it.

He had a feeling Ryker was right. He'd already figured out that Christy was different from anyone he'd ever dated. She was still more suspicious than impressed with his fancy apartment and its fancy address. Although she had gotten positively dewy-eyed when she'd seen the guest suite bathroom.

He shrugged a shoulder. What could he expect? Cara Lynn had told him no woman could resist it. Apparently not even the woman Ryker had dubbed the Ice Queen.

An erotic image of Christy in his guest bathroom, enveloped in steam and nothing else, rose in his vision. With a considerable effort, he banished it and forced his thoughts back to her secrecy and lies.

The way she carried that shoulder bag clutched against her as if she were protecting it with her life, he was sure that whatever she'd found in her sister's secret hiding place, it was in that bag. And he needed to get his hands on it.

Chapter Eleven

Reilly put his hand on the doorknob and called out again. "Christy?"

No answer. It didn't take him ten seconds to make his decision. He was going in. If she caught him, he'd tell her he had supper ready. If she was still in the bathroom, he was going to go through her purse. He was a law enforcement officer. If the bag was in plain view and he had reasonable cause—

He didn't even try to make that argument, not even to himself. It was too flimsy. He was snooping, but it was for her own good, damn it. She was meddling in danger she didn't understand, and if he didn't do something, she was going to get herself killed.

He couldn't sit by and let that happen.

He eased open the door and stepped into the suite. It was empty. The bathroom lights were on and the scent of gardenias wafted across his nostrils, rekindling the erotic images in his brain. The images were enhanced by Christy's voice. She was humming. The sweet low melody reverberated in his ears.

He breathed deeply, letting the scent permeate his every pore and her voice penetrate his brain. Then he scowled.

Stop it. He didn't have much time. He needed to see what was in her purse. What she was keeping from him. He spotted the slouchy shoulder bag sitting on a chair near the dresser, on the far side of the room. He glanced at the doorway into the bath. If she was still in the tub, and he was pretty sure she was, she had her back to the doorway. He just hoped she was planning to soak for at least another five minutes or so.

He tiptoed toward the chair—and ran straight into Christy. She'd come out just in time to slam into him.

She shrieked.

He yelped. He teetered, caught himself then grabbed her shoulders to keep her from falling.

"What are you—?"

"Hey, I—"

Both of them stopped. And again, they spoke at the same time.

"What are you—?"

"I didn't mean—"

Christy's damp hair was tickling Reilly's nose, and the heady fragrance of gardenias enveloped him. Her breasts were pressed against his arm. When he looked down, he saw that she was dressed in nothing but a towel. A warm, damp towel that didn't disguise the rounded firmness of her breasts at all. He took a step backwards and gaped at her.

She pressed a hand against the top of the towel in surprise and confusion. "What are you doing?" she asked.

"I—" he started, stammering. "Dinner's ready."

"Dinner?"

"I thought you'd be done by now."

Christy's lashes were wet and stuck together, forming black starbursts around her green eyes. The cut on her cheek was healing, and the bruise had turned that ugly greenish-yellow color.

Reilly did his best to keep his gaze on her beautiful eyes, but he wasn't strong enough. He couldn't resist looking down again, at the top of her breasts, barely covered by the towel. Her hand was still pressing there. His mouth went dry.

Then his gaze was caught by something strange on her arm. Dark marks, several of them. Five, to be exact. Four on the bicep and one on the inner curve of her tricep.

"What the hell?" he snapped, reaching out a hand.

She recoiled.

"Christy, what happened?"

Christy frowned at him then followed his gaze to her left upper arm. Her other hand with the pink cast wrapped tightly in plastic wrap, rose as if to cover the marks.

He held up his hand, fingers spread, and matched his fingertips to the marks without actually touching her skin. Some bastard had grabbed her—hurt her. His certainty came from too many domestic violence 911 calls.

"Who did this?" He heard his deadly quiet, commanding tone.

She met his gaze and her face drained of color.

Ah, hell. There was a reason Ryker called his furious expression "The Silencer." Reilly had seen its effect on criminals and once or twice on his twin brother and cousins.

Regret washed over him, and he worked to compose his face. "I didn't mean to scare you," he said gently. He wasn't mad at her. At least not very. He was furious with whoever had grabbed her. Although, once he found out where she'd been to be subjected to that kind of violence, he might be furious at her.

She didn't say anything, but fat tears welled in her eyes. She blinked, and two of them slid over the lids and rolled down her cheeks.

Then her lips moved.

It took him a minute to decipher what she was trying to say. Her voice had failed her, so he had to read her lips. "I'm sorry." And again, "I'm sorry."

For one microsecond, he wished he could grab her and

jerk some sense into her, as his grandmother had always threatened to do to Ryker and him.

But the only time his grandmother had ever actually laid a hand on him was when he was eight and he'd chased his cousin Cara Lynn with a stick. Grandmother had pinched his ear. *I ought to jerk some sense into you,* she'd said. *You don't hit girls. Not with sticks. Not with anything. You don't even threaten to. You are a boy. You're stronger than a girl. Your job is to protect them, not hurt them.*

He'd taken her words to heart. He had never and would never touch a woman in anger. Certainly not Christy. Not that creamy, beautiful skin. He loved it, longed to soothe it, to kiss away the angry bruises.

As his thoughts swirled, something happened inside him. Something he'd been fighting against ever since he'd first laid eyes on Christy Moser. He'd been telling himself that his only purpose was to help her, to protect her. But now, as the scent of gardenias wafted across his nostrils and sent desire burning through his loins, he realized she wasn't the only one who'd been lying.

He'd been lying too—to himself. He'd been ignoring the erotic dreams that haunted him every night and lingered long after he woke up. He'd been doing his best to deny the need that burned in him each time he was close to her. That burned in him now.

The curve of her bare shoulders, her breasts, pushed into luscious fullness by the tightly wrapped towel, her damp eyes and red nose all forced him to admit how much he wanted her.

And that face. The high cheekbones, the wide mouth, those lips—not too full, but sensual.

He felt himself stir, grow, rub painfully against his jeans. He wanted to kiss her. He *needed* to kiss her.

Now.

His fingers still hovered over the marred skin of her arm. He left his hand there and lifted his right hand. He held it close to her bare back, so close he could feel the heat from her skin on his palm. There was something wildly erotic about being so close to her and not touching her.

He leaned in and touched his mouth to hers. Just a light, feathery brushing of lips against lips. That soft whisper was the only place their bodies touched each other.

After what seemed to him like an eternity, Reilly dared to lean in a little more. He deepened the kiss, just barely. He liked this. They were welded together, not because he was holding her or she was clinging to him. They were joined by nothing more than an impossibly tender kiss.

He'd started it, yes. But she was responding. She was holding him in thrall as much as he was her.

When she lifted her arms and, with a torturous slowness, laid her palms against his chest where his long-sleeved shirt hung open, his breath caught sharply. Her fingers were hot, the plastic wrap she'd covered her cast with was wet. It spilled a few drops of water down his chest. He shivered. His skin pebbled with goose bumps. His nipples tightened and Christy brushed them with her fingertips.

He grew instantly hard, burning with the need to strain, to rub himself against her. It would be agonizing through his clothes, but he didn't care.

No. He needed to control himself. She'd been hurt. It wasn't fair to her to take advantage of her vulnerability. He pulled back and squeezed his eyes closed for a moment.

"Christy," he growled. "This isn't—"

"Don't," she whispered. "Don't talk. You'll ruin everything." She lifted an edge of the plastic wrap and unwrapped it from around her cast, loosing rivulets of water. She let it drop to the floor and turned back to him.

She ran her hands up, across his collarbone to his neck.

The edge of her cast scratched the tender area underneath his jaw, sending more goose bumps skittering across his skin. He groaned.

Then she wrapped her arms around his neck and pulled him to her. As she did, the towel around her body loosened and fell to the floor. Reilly's last vestige of self-control fell right alongside it. He'd been fighting this attraction for days. He couldn't resist it, not now.

Finally, he touched her. The bare, marred skin of her arm, the firm curve of her back. He traced the hills and valleys of her exquisitely feminine body the way he'd longed to do ever since he'd first set eyes on her in the courthouse lobby.

He hadn't admitted, even to himself, how much he'd longed to touch her, to hold her like this. He'd almost begun to believe that there was nothing between them.

Almost.

But now, as she tugged at his shirt, trying to push it down his arms, murmuring her frustration because she couldn't grasp the thin material with her cast-wrapped hand, he gave in to the fierce attraction that burned in him like a bonfire.

He moved them closer to the bed as he brushed her fumbling hands away and shed the shirt. Then he made quick work of his jeans.

Gently, tamping down on his own need, he urged her down on the bed and lay beside her, drawing her into his arms. He kissed her deeply and pressed the full length of his body against hers.

She moaned his name and arched toward him as his erection pressed against the apex of her thighs. He rocked his hips, pushing against her again and again. At the same time, he bent his head and ran his tongue along the swell of her breasts, first one and then the other. Teasing, circling, but not touching, their distended tips.

Christy entangled her fingers in his hair and held him

there at one full, swelling breast. Finally he took the tiny bud in his mouth, suckling and nipping at it until her breath hitched. Then he moved to the other breast, giving its peak the same attention. Her uneven, gasping breaths fueled his own desire to a fever pitch. He wasn't sure how much longer he could hold on to his control. He needed her so badly.

As if he'd spoken aloud, she slid her hand down across his abs and lower.

"Ah," he breathed and looked down. A faint red mark followed the line of her hand.

"Oh, no!" she exclaimed, withdrawing her hand. "I can't—my cast is scratching you."

He lifted her hand and kissed the fingers. "That's okay. Put your arms around my neck."

She did, and he wrapped his arms around her and hooked one leg around hers, then he flipped them over, putting her on his left. "Now," he muttered, smiling at her.

Using her left hand, she followed the same path down his body, following her fingers with her lips, kissing the reddened skin. He gasped aloud and threw his head back. The feel of her lips feathering across his abs, his belly and his lower abdomen nearly undid him. His erection jumped as her fingers slid across his length and then wrapped around him.

He thrust against her palm. His breaths came short and hard. But he knew this wasn't fair. He was taking pleasure, not giving it. He gritted his teeth and urged her to look at him. "You've got to slow down, Doc," he muttered.

Then he trailed his fingers down her belly and dipped into her core. She was slick and flowing, ready for him. His breath caught.

He kissed her, using the kiss to urge her head back onto the pillow, using his hands to spread her legs apart. He lifted himself and let her guide him into her.

The hot, tight feel of her made him utter a cry as he sank

into her as deeply as he could. Her cry echoed his. He thrust then withdrew slowly, thrust and withdrew, until Christy's breaths were as short and sharp as his.

He breathed harshly, clenching his jaw, trying to last as long as he possibly could—which, from the way he felt, wasn't going to be very long at all.

"Reilly, please," she begged. He lifted his head and met her gaze. Her eyelids were heavy, her mouth open as her chest rose and fell with her quick breaths.

"I'm trying to—make it last," he said.

"Don't," she breathed against his mouth. "Not on my account." Then she nipped his lower lip and kissed him deeply and long.

But he still tried, his jaw aching, his entire being filled with the exquisite pain of nearly impossible restraint.

Then, just as he thought he couldn't hold out another second, he felt the change in her rhythm. No longer was she smooth and languid, twisting her sinuous body beneath his. She stiffened, then her breath caught and she moaned, a sweet, low sound of bliss.

His heart thrilled. She'd found her pleasure. Her breath caught, her body strained, then, as he held his breath and thrust one more time, she reached her pinnacle.

A low, guttural cry and a series of painfully sweet spasms triggered his own climax. He came hard and long, his release seeming to last and last. Finally exhausted, he lowered himself beside her, pulling her into the curve of his arm. Their ragged breathing pulsed in rhythm, their muscles quivered in unison.

Reilly inhaled Christy's scent as he waited for the last minuscule aftershocks of orgasm to fade. He lay, eyes closed, basking in the delicious weariness of his body.

He felt drained. Totally satisfied and yet at the same time hungry for more. More of Christy's unaffected passion. More of that delicious heat, that exquisite tightness that he didn't think he would ever tire of exploring.

He opened his eyes and in the plane of his vision was her bruised arm. Slowly, as if crawling out of a murky creek, the memory of those bruises emerged.

As did his questions. His languorous afterglow faded, and he crashed back into the real world. The world where she was lying to him at every turn, concealing dangerous evidence and venturing out alone to confront people who had hurt her. The world where he was becoming convinced that the man who had killed Christy's sister and wanted to kill her was one of his own. A fellow police officer.

CHRISTY WOKE UP FEELING more relaxed than she had in a long, long time. She squinted at the clock on the bedside table. It was five in the morning. They hadn't gone to sleep until after twelve, so she'd only slept about five hours. Not nearly enough.

She stretched. The coolness on her skin and the silence that surrounded her told her she was alone. She felt the pillow beside her. It was indented, but the cotton was cool. Reilly had been gone a long time.

She sat up, fluffing a pillow behind her back and pulling the sheet up with her to cover her nakedness. Reaching out, she turned on the bedside lamp. Was Reilly one of those people who couldn't sleep with someone else in the bed? Or had he regretted what they'd done and gone back to his own room in order to avoid her?

She stopped that thought. She wasn't going to think about why he wasn't in the bed at five o'clock in the morning. It didn't matter. Not yet.

Right now she was still relaxed and languid, basking in the afterglow of really great sex. A small pinprick of pain shot along the skin of her right upper arm. She rubbed it. It was sore to the touch.

Glancing down at the dark bruises, she remembered Reilly's reaction. He'd been so angry. At first she'd thought he was furious at her, but then she'd realized his anger, while scary, wasn't a threat to her. He was angry at the person who had hurt her.

She'd almost lost it when he'd asked her who had put the bruises there. She'd wanted so badly to confess everything to him and let him handle Jazzy and Glo. He was a policeman. He knew how to deal with people like that, how to make them tell the truth. And he knew how to make people like her feel safe.

No. She couldn't think like that. The fact that Reilly made her feel safe scared her. From what she was learning, it appeared that one of Reilly's fellow officers may have killed Autumn.

How would he react if she told him that? Everything she knew about the police, everything she'd seen when her mother was killed, told her that when threatened, cops closed ranks. They formed the famous blue line she'd heard about. They protected their own.

Reilly wouldn't buy that argument. He'd gone into law enforcement because he wanted to set things right. She had no doubt of that. He was that kind of person. His honor, his integrity, shone in those intense blue eyes and in the pride with which he wore the uniform.

For that very reason, she knew she couldn't tell him what she'd found. He'd insist on turning in the evidence, just like he had the money and drugs, confident that no matter whom it implicated, they would be brought to justice.

But Christy was terrified that once the evidence was out of her possession, she'd lose any chance she had to solve her sister's murder. So, until she had incontrovertible proof in her hands, and maybe an attorney by her side, she wasn't telling anybody about Autumn's SIM card, the brass button or the note.

She turned off the lamp and slid down in the bed to sleep some more. After a few minutes of tossing and turning as her thoughts swirled around in her brain like leaves in a whirlwind, she threw the covers back and got up.

Where were her clothes? She looked around and spotted the white towel in a puddle on the floor. That's right. She hadn't been wearing any.

Her cheeks flamed as she hurried over to her suitcase and grabbed underwear and a loose rayon lounging outfit and darted into the bathroom to shower.

When she stepped into the living room, Reilly was sitting in the same place as he'd been early yesterday morning. Sitting at the dining room table with several file folders spread in front of him and a steaming mug beside his right hand. He was dressed in the worn jeans he'd had on last night, and that was all. His torso and his feet were bare.

She couldn't move, couldn't breathe. Sitting there, unaware that she was watching him, he was unconsciously, carelessly beautiful. His skin glowed like gold in the early morning light. He had a lean, rugged strength about him that made her feel safe just because he was here. But safe wasn't the only thing she felt. Desire pooled in her deepest core at the sight of his long, firm muscles, his silk-over-steel skin, his mouth that was made for kissing.

He was a cut above anyone she'd ever dated. His lovemaking had left her exhausted and tingling. He'd been forceful, yes, but also tender. Perfection.

Suddenly she realized he'd stopped what he was doing and was looking up at her. She met his gaze, a small smile growing on her face.

"Morning," he said, his expression friendly but neutral. It

could have been yesterday, or any other day that they hadn't spent the night making love. "You really shouldn't be up. You need a few more hours of sleep."

"Don't you?" she countered, her smile fading. She'd expected something—a morning kiss, maybe an embrace. Something to verify that last night had been more than just sex.

Reilly lifted his arms above his head and arched his spine in a stretch. "Ahh," he yawned. "I could sleep some more, but I've got things I need to do."

Things that obviously were more important than what they'd experienced together. Fine. He'd found her in nothing but a towel, and naturally, they'd fallen into bed together.

Christy winced. She didn't like that kind of hookup. For her, sex needed to be more than just physical attraction.

Apparently Reilly was more typical male than she'd thought.

He picked up his mug and took a swallow, then eyed her. "Are you hungry? We sort of skipped dinner."

"I am." She turned from him and looked into the kitchen. "And I smell coffee."

"Get some and in a few minutes I'll make scrambled eggs."

"That's okay. I'll make something," she offered. "Have you got bread?"

He grinned over the top of his mug. "Like I told you. I've got everything."

"Good." Christy found half a loaf of French bread. She squeezed it. Stale—perfect. She sliced it, soaked it in a bowl of beaten eggs and a dollop of the cream Reilly used in his coffee, sprinkled it with cinnamon and fried it in butter.

While she was waiting for the French toast, or *pain perdu* as the Cajuns called it, she watched Reilly across the kitchen island.

He seemed completely absorbed in the folders and papers before him. Did they concern her sister's death? She decided to wait until after breakfast to ask him.

When the French toast was ready, she set two pieces on a plate for her and arranged four on Reilly's plate. There was a jar of maple syrup in the pantry and orange marmalade in the refrigerator.

By the time she had the plates on the island with the syrup and marmalade beside them, Reilly had picked up his mug, refilled it and sat on one of the barstools.

"This looks great," he said. He poured maple syrup over the toast and dug in.

She watched him. Even shoveling food into his mouth, he was so beautiful, so graceful and at the same time so masculine, that it made her heart ache.

After a few bites, he looked up at her. "Aren't you going to eat?"

She nodded. Her mug sat next to her hand, forgotten. She picked it up and rounded the island to sit next to him on one of the leather-cushioned barstools.

The French toast, which she ate with orange marmalade, was good, even if she hadn't been able to find any cardamom, which she thought added a surprising savory bite to it. By the time she'd finished hers, Reilly had sat back and was draining his coffee.

"Wow," he said. "That was almost as good as my grandmother's. You used the stale French bread?"

She nodded.

"You used cream? Lots of butter? Yep. That's the perfect recipe."

He leaned toward her and gave her a maple syrupy peck on the lips. "Thank you," he murmured, pressing his forehead to hers for an instant.

Then he was up and gone, around the island to wash his

hands and rinse the syrup off his mouth, then back to the dining room table.

Christy cleaned up the kitchen in record time, poured herself a second mug of coffee and joined him, sitting to his left.

"I meant to ask you if you saw Deputy Watts yesterday. Had he found out anything?"

Reilly slid his chair slightly away from her. Giving her room, or avoiding being too close?

"Matter of fact, yeah," he said, glancing at her sidelong. He pushed his chair back a little more and faced her, his expression a cross between earnest and grim.

Christy's heart began to pound. He'd found out something. She pressed a hand to her chest.

"The bullet we dug out of the wall matched the bullets that killed your sister."

Chapter Twelve

Christy's hand flew to her heart because she thought it might stop. "Th-the bullets matched?"

Reilly was watching her closely. After a moment, he continued. "There's more. The fingerprint on the shell casing CSI picked up outside your window at the inn was a fourteen-point match to a small-time dealer named Buddy Kramer."

Christy's hand moved to cover her mouth. "Kramer?" she whispered.

Reilly's eyes narrowed. "You know him?"

She shook her head. Could she lie with those eyes on her? She wanted so badly to tell him the truth. But the leaves were swirling in her brain again. She had to have time to process what he was telling her. Right now, she couldn't think.

"I—no. No, of course not. Did you mention him?"

He shook his head without taking his eyes off her.

"B-because—" she stammered, "it sounds familiar."

"It sounds familiar," he repeated, his tone flat. She didn't have to guess why. He didn't believe her. "Where have you heard it? From your sister?"

She swallowed, making a conscious effort to continue breathing. "Maybe. He's a drug dealer?"

Reilly's gaze finally unlocked from hers. He glanced down at one of the folders in front of him. "According to Watts. He's not a major player. He hangs out somewhere around the old Hotel Winsor in downtown Mandeville and sells drugs to street crud."

Glo had mentioned the Hotel Winsor. Christy's pulse jack-hammered. "Why—" She had to take a breath. "Why isn't he in jail, if the police know what he's doing? What kind of police work is that?"

"I know this isn't going to make much sense to you, but Kramer is a CI."

"A CI?"

Reilly nodded. "Confidential informant. Some of the detectives have them. Most often it's vice. But homicide detectives use them too."

His words confirmed her distrust of the police. "And they let them roam around free? Selling drugs and—" she waved a hand "—pimping and whatever, so they can inform on other crooks?" She knew her voice was dripping with incredulity and disgust. But that was okay, because that was how she felt—shocked and disgusted.

Reilly didn't comment.

"So this Buddy Kramer probably murdered my sister," she continued, "and now he's shooting at me with the same gun, and nothing can be done because one of *your* detective buddies is protecting him. I'm so glad that my trust and confidence in the police is not misplaced."

Reilly looked taken aback. It occurred to her that she hadn't actually explained to him she didn't trust the police, although he should have figured it out by now.

"Hey, Doc. I'm not defending the practice. But information from informants has led to some major drug busts. Illegal drug operations are like fire ants. You destroy a hill here and they just move over there and build again. So putting away a small-time dealer is like trying to destroy a fire ant hill by killing one ant."

Christy felt like crying. Like hitting something—or

someone. "I am so glad to know you *don't defend the practice.* Don't you get it? I don't *care* about your drug busts or your informants or—or your metaphors right now. Buddy Kramer may have killed my sister. He's shooting at me. And the police aren't going to do anything. *That* is all I care about."

She pushed her chair back and stood. "There has to be somebody who will help me. Maybe I'll go see the sheriff himself."

Reilly stood too. "Listen to me. Nobody is going to let Kramer walk if he murdered your sister or tried to kill you. We have evidence that he handled the casing of the bullet that was shot at you. That'll get him brought in for questioning."

"Questioning." Christy gave a harsh laugh. "That makes me feel better."

Reilly laid a hand on her arm. "Come on. Calm down. Watts is picking up Kramer today. They'll lean on him hard. But that print on the casing is the only evidence they've got against him, and it's circumstantial."

Christy didn't want Reilly touching her. When he stood so close to her and touched her with his strong, capable hands, she was tempted to believe every word that dropped from his lips.

She picked up her mug and took it into the kitchen, more to get away from him than any concern for neatness.

"Circumstantial. Something else I never understood. On the cop shows it just sounds like an excuse to let a guilty person walk."

Reilly walked around the island and propped a hip against it. "We feel that way too, a lot of times. The law is designed to avoid convicting an innocent person, so from this side, it looks ridiculously easy for a guilty person to walk. But that's the way it is, and that's what we have to deal with. Innocent until proven guilty." He held up his forefinger. "Guilty beyond a reasonable doubt." He raised a second finger.

She glared at him. "So finding the casing with Kramer's fingerprint on it outside my window right after a bullet barely missed me isn't enough to prove he did it?"

He shook his head, looking genuinely chagrined. "Nope. It just proves that he touched the bullet at some point. It would help a lot if we'd found something that proved he was there."

Christy threw up her hands. "Why doesn't his fingerprint on the bullet prove he was there?"

Reilly sighed. "Guns get passed around. Bullets too. Although it's hard to believe even a lowlife like Kramer would be stupid enough not to wear gloves while loading a magazine." He shrugged. "Or that he'd keep a gun with a body on it."

Anger bubbled up in Christy's chest, making her eyes sting with tears. "A body on it? That *body* was my sister."

To his credit, Reilly's face turned red and he looked chagrined. "I'm sorry. I shouldn't have said it like that."

"But you did." She held up her hands, palm out. "Please don't tell me that it's a coincidence that a bullet touched by the man who killed my sister was the one that was shot at me."

He ducked his head. "Yeah. When you put it that way, it doesn't sound very plausible."

"No, it doesn't. So are you going with Deputy Watts to pick up Kramer?"

"Me? No. It's not my jurisdiction, but I'm planning to be there when he interviews him."

"I want to go too."

Reilly's brows shot up. "Hell, no. You're not going anywhere. Certainly not anywhere near Buddy Kramer. Am I going to have to get a court order to put you into protective custody?"

"You wouldn't dare." But she knew by the look on his face that he would.

"Don't tempt me. If I can't depend on you to stay put, I'll do it in a heartbeat. I need your word that you're not going to go running around getting into trouble. Hasn't it penetrated that thick skull of yours that someone wants you dead?"

"Of course it has. I'm reminded of it every day." She held up her hand with the cast on it.

A faraway chime sounded. Christy listened. It was Autumn's phone. She started past him, but he caught her arm.

"What's that?" Reilly asked.

"My phone." She pulled away.

He shook his head. "No, it's not. That's not your ring."

Christy swallowed. "Of course it is. I—changed it." She pushed past him again, but he held on. Not hard. Just enough that she knew he wanted a straight answer.

"When are you going to quit lying to me, Christy?"

AUTUMN'S PHONE CHIMED again. Christy extracted her arm from Reilly's grip. "When are you going to quit protecting murderers and criminals and actually do something about catching the man who killed my sister?"

She turned and ran for the phone, which was in her purse in the guest room. It had to be Glo or Laurie calling with more information. She couldn't afford to miss the call.

The phone stopped ringing just as she managed to wrap her hand around it.

"Oh, no," she muttered. She dug it out and looked at the display. It was Glo's number.

"Who was it?"

Reilly's voice came from the open doorway of the guest suite. Christy half turned, putting her back to the door, and dropped the phone back into her purse. Then she lifted her head and turned around. "I didn't get to it in time, but it was an unknown number." She shrugged.

He took a step into the room. "Maybe they left a message."

"No. No message."

Shaking his head, Reilly looked down at the floor then back up at her. "Damn it, Christy. Tell me the truth for once. I thought you'd figured out by now that I'm the good guy. What you said before about the police, I don't know why you feel you can't trust us, but whatever it is—"

"You don't know?" she broke in. "I'm amazed that it's not in my file."

"Your file? What are you talking about? You mean the report Ryker gave me about his interview with you?"

"Oh, come on. It had to have come up."

"What had to have come up? What are you talking about?"

Looking at his face, she realized he didn't know. She crossed her arms across her chest and faced him. "Let me enlighten you."

"I wish you would. A rational explanation for how you've been acting would be nice. I'm sick of you lying to me. I know you are, just like I know you're withholding evidence that could probably help us find your sister's killer."

"Fine." Christy rubbed her temple, squeezing her eyes shut at the slight relief it gave her from the headache that had been hovering there.

"My mother died when I was sixteen and Autumn was twelve. She was a professor at Loyola. A tenured professor. Very well thought of."

Reilly nodded.

"Do you remember the student protests on campus back in the '90s?" She stopped and waited for his answer.

"Yeah. I was in high school. Ryker and I and a couple of friends drove down there that night. We wanted to practice our detective skills. See if we could find any blood or—" He stopped and his expression turned to shock. "Oh, God, Christy—"

"I thought you'd get it. There were three people shot by the police who responded. Two died. A student who rushed a cop, and a woman who just happened to be in the wrong place at the wrong time."

"Damn," Reilly whispered.

"My mother, according to the girl who was standing beside her, was giving her directions to the library. A bullet grazed the girl in the head, and my mother took two in the back."

"Christy, I'm—"

She held up a hand. "Save it. You haven't heard what the police told my dad, my sister and me. It's the best part. They said, 'These things happen.'" She took a sharp breath. "Oh, and, 'Your mother died bravely.'"

"I'm sure she did—"

"Please!" Christy burst out. "She didn't die bravely. She died pitifully, crumpled on the grass and alone." Her voice caught and she had to clear her throat. "But that wasn't all. The police commissioner made sure to tell us, 'You'll be glad to know that we caught the students who attacked the policemen.'"

"That's awful," Reilly said. "I can't tell you how sorry I am. Didn't you get a settlement of some kind—?"

"A settlement? Of course. The city bestowed a few thousand dollars on my father. Do you think that even began to make up for what my mother's death did to my family? For my sister getting involved in drugs and dying? My father killing those women? My—" She waved a hand.

After a moment she continued. "Do you know that not once did anyone offer to tell us who had shot my mother? Or why he'd fired toward innocent people. Nothing ever happened to that policeman. And why? Because the police protect their own. Whoever killed my mother is still carrying a badge and a gun. Still *keeping the peace.* So hopefully you'll understand if I'm not the biggest fan of the police. From where I stand, it's a little hard to tell the good guys from the bad."

Reilly hadn't moved. He looked a bit shell-shocked. "I told you before, Christy. I'm a good guy."

Christy's heart twisted. She knew that. Ever since this whole nightmare began, Reilly had been the one constant in her suddenly out-of-control life. The one person she could trust.

Standing there in the doorway, tall and strong and handsome, he looked like everything she'd ever wanted. She was so tempted to throw herself into his arms and tell him everything. Let him take the whole burden of finding out who'd murdered Autumn.

But he was a cop. That one thing stopped her every time.

The tiny bit of evidence she had wasn't enough. She had to find something more, something that proved beyond a shadow of a doubt who the cop was that had given Autumn drugs. Because she was sure that when she found that man, she'd have Autumn's murderer.

Right now, her only lead was the small-time dealer, Buddy Kramer. And to get to him, she had to go through Glo.

She resisted putting a hand over her aching heart and leveled a flat gaze at Reilly. "If you'll excuse me, I need to get dressed."

Reilly's eyes left her face and flickered downward, toward her purse. "Where are you going?" he asked.

"To see my father, of course," she responded.

Reilly looked back at her. "Christy—"

"Don't, Reilly."

His face went dark, his eyes changed and his fists clenched at his side. "I wish I could jerk some sense into you. You're going to get yourself killed."

He aimed a razor-sharp glare at her. "I don't know why I care. All you've done is block me at every turn and tell me you don't need me. If I thought I could get away with it, I'd lock you up so fast your head would spin."

Christy stared at him, unable to speak. A chill ran down her spine at his hard tone.

He stood there for a few seconds, then lifted his hands, palms out. "Go ahead. Do what you want. I give up."

He turned on his heel and left the room.

Christy stared at the empty doorway. Suddenly her chest felt hollow and sore, as if he'd ripped out her heart and taken it with him. She looked down at her hands. They were trembling. Her legs too, so badly she wasn't sure they'd hold her up. It was as if Reilly had been her strength. She'd thought she was doing this on her own. That she was strong enough, tough enough, to find her sister's killer. But whether she'd been willing to admit it or not, Reilly had had her back the whole time, giving her strength and courage.

Now, he'd given up on her. She really was on her own. And suddenly, she wasn't so confident.

By the time Christy came out of her room dressed in black slacks and a black-and-white block-print sweater, Reilly was dressed and waiting for her. He sat at the dining room table, pretending to be engrossed in the files before him, but the sheets of paper were a blur as his thoughts raced.

He wasn't sure he was ready for this. In the past hour, he'd tried to examine every possible scenario, but he'd kept coming back to the same plan. It was dangerous, maybe even foolish, especially given the evidence before him. As he'd told Ryker, the more he learned, the more convinced he was that Autumn's secret boyfriend was a cop—the drugs with police evidence markings on it, the fact that a known CI's fingerprint was on the gun used to kill Autumn Moser and shoot at Christy Moser. Not to mention his certainty that Christy was holding back evidence. Evidence she'd found among Autumn's things. Evidence that very likely implicated a cop.

Given how her mother had died, he could understand why she was reluctant to trust him or anyone else on the police force.

It pissed him off, but he could understand it.

Christy cleared her throat softly. Reilly sucked in a deep breath and looked up, as if he'd just realized she was there. "I talked to Deputy Watts a few minutes ago. He dragged Buddy Kramer in for questioning early this morning."

Christy looked at him wide-eyed. "What did he find out?"

Reilly shook his head. "Not much. Buddy swore he had no idea how his fingerprint got on that shell casing. Said he was playing poker the night you were shot at. Has four friends who can alibi him."

"But he's lying! Isn't he?"

"Probably. Still, like I told you, without any trace evidence or the gun itself, there's not much we can do."

"What do you mean, not much?"

Reilly shrugged. "Watts had to let him go."

"No!" Christy cried, her face reflecting disbelief. "He can't. Don't they have something else they can hold him on until they get enough evidence? I mean, he's a drug dealer, right?"

"He is, but there's no point in holding him for something unrelated to the shooting. Even if they did have a specific possession or intent-to-distribute charge, that wouldn't help your case." Reilly glanced down. "And it could ruin a sting operation that's been working for months to track down the drug distributor. Maybe even the smuggler who imports them."

Christy's eyes sparkled with unshed tears. "This is so frustrating! Can you blame me for not trusting the police?"

"I can understand how you feel, but—" He spread his hands, as if to say, *What can you do?*

Then he took a deep breath and glanced down casually at the papers in front of him. "So, are you going to catch a taxi to the hospital today?" he asked, forcing an even, detached tone into his voice. He risked a peek at her face.

She looked surprised. "A taxi? You want me to call a taxi?"

He shrugged. "I may go to my mom's for Sunday dinner. As a matter of fact, you might want to rent a car. I'm going back to work Monday." The lie tasted like gall in his mouth, but it was necessary to his plan. God, he hoped he was doing the right thing.

Christy's head jerked slightly, as if from a blow. "I—I can do that. I'll do it today." She reached into her purse for her phone. "I should probably go to a hotel too." Her voice sounded small, a bit hurt.

Reilly had expected that. "That's not necessary. My maid comes tomorrow though, so you might want to put away anything you wouldn't want her to see."

He watched her as she started to speak, stopped and swallowed, then opened her mouth again. "I will. Thanks for letting me know." She turned around and walked back into the guest suite. As soon as he heard her on the phone, ordering a taxi, he grabbed his phone and called his brother Dawson.

"Hi, Reilly," Dawson said when he picked up. "You going to be at Mom's for lunch today?"

"Nope. I'm sort of on a case. In fact, that's why I called. I need a GPS tracker for a car." Reilly watched the door of the guest suite as he talked.

"Since when does SWAT tail people?"

"This is kind of a personal favor."

"Sure. You want to pick it up this afternoon?"

Reilly sat up. "Actually, I need it now. Think you can run it by here? Leave it behind the right rear tire of my car?"

There was a brief silence. "You don't ask for much, do you?"

"Thanks, Dawson. I owe you one."

"You owe me several, but who's counting?"

Reilly hung up and wiped a hand down his face. Damn, he hated being so deceptive. But short of kicking Christy out, locking her up or holding her at gunpoint while he went through her things, it was the only way he knew to find out what she was holding back.

He'd thought about requesting a tail for her, but had decided against it. He'd started this, and he was going to finish it. Besides, the way things were going, he wasn't willing to trust Christy's safety to anyone else.

He just hoped to hell she decided to rent a car instead of using taxis. He doubted a taxi driver would appreciate having a GPS tracker attached to his vehicle. As soon as he tapped her car, he needed to call Deputy Chief Mike Davis and fill him in on what he was doing, in case he needed backup.

Mike wasn't going to like it. Hell, it could be the end of Reilly's career, but that couldn't be helped. His career wouldn't be worth squat if he let Christy get herself killed. He planned to be right behind her, wherever she went.

AFTER CHRISTY PICKED UP a rental car, she drove to the hospital to see her father. On the way, she called Glo. The girl's voice was just as smoky and raspy as it had been before.

"Glo, it's Christy. Christy Moser. You called me earlier?"

"Yeah. I've got more information. I wondered if you—you know—had some more money for me."

Christy winced. She didn't want to go inside Glo's house again. "What kind of information?"

"It's good. It might help you with—you know—your sister."

"All right," Christy said reluctantly. "Do you want me to come down there?"

"No," Glo said quickly. "I'll meet you, but I don't have a car, so it can't be—you know—too far."

"Just tell me where."

"Do you know the old shopping center on Middle Street? There used to be a drug store on the corner called Brent's."

"I can find it."

"I'll be there at the corner by the drug store."

"What time?" As Christy spoke, she heard noise in the background. Was it Jazzy yelling?

"Two o'clock," Glo whispered and hung up.

Christy pulled into the parking lot at the hospital and sat with the motor running as she entered Middle Street, Chef Voleur, LA, into the car's built-in GPS locator. The device indicated that it would take her nineteen minutes to get there. She decided she should allow forty-five, since she didn't know how long Middle Street was or where on the street the shopping center was located.

She got to the cardiac care unit just in time for noon visitation. Her dad seemed to be struggling to breathe, and she didn't like the gray tint to his skin. She spoke to him and kissed him on the cheek, but as usual, he didn't respond. Quickly, she glanced at the IV fluids that were hanging. They'd increased the morphine drip, and his lidocaine had been upped too. She looked at the heart monitor. His heart beat was irregular.

She swallowed hard and tried to choke back the tears that clogged her throat. He was getting worse. Sometimes, like right now, she hated being a doctor. Because her knowledge told her that her father wasn't going to survive much longer. His life was now being measured in days, if not hours. She took his hand in hers. "I'm sorry, Daddy."

Chapter Thirteen

"I'm so sorry. I should have been here," Christy whispered to her dad.

The sound of a throat clearing caught her attention. "Dr. Moser."

She turned. It was the cardiologist. She smiled. "Please call me Christy."

Dr. Tanner gave the IVs and the monitor a cursory glance. Then he looked down at the chart he held in his hand. "Only if you'll call me Jim."

"He's worse," she said. Not a question.

Jim nodded. "He's lost some ground since yesterday."

She nodded, swallowing again.

"We can still hope that he'll turn around, but as I told you the other day, with the amount of damage to his heart muscle, he's just not pumping enough blood. And that blood doesn't have enough oxygen."

"I know," she said, nodding. "But I'm sure you realize, there's a difference in being a doctor and being a daughter. So forgive me if I'm in daughter mode right now."

He smiled back. "I do understand. Did your father have a living will?"

"No. As far as I know, he never wrote one." She sighed. "He was never sick."

"I see. We should discuss your options. Soon."

Soon. The word cut into her heart. She'd known for a couple of days now that her father was never coming out of the hospital, but hearing it from the cardiologist still hurt.

"I want you to know that if we put a *do not resuscitate* order into the chart, that won't affect his care at all. The only thing that will change is that if he goes into cardiac arrest—"

"I know. I agree." She squeezed her dad's hand.

Dr. Tanner nodded gravely. "I'll have the nurse prepare the paperwork for you to sign. And Christy—"

She looked at him.

"I'll let the nurses know that you can come in anytime to see him and stay as long as you like."

"Thank you, Jim. I appreciate it."

Christy spent an hour with her dad, holding his hand and talking to him, even though he was too heavily sedated to respond. Then she headed to her rental car and followed the directions to Middle Street in Chef Voleur. On the way, she stopped at an ATM and withdrew several hundred dollars. She folded five twenties and stuck them in the pocket of her sweater, then put the rest in her purse.

It didn't take her long to find the shopping center and the drug store. As Glo had warned her, the place was abandoned.

Christy was fifteen minutes early. Once she saw the condition of the neighborhood, she decided not to stop.

When she drove past the drug store for the third time, she saw Glo huddled against the storefront near the corner. A car pulled up with the passenger window lowered. Glo bent down slightly as if listening, then shook her head. A second or two later she shook her head again, said something and made a gesture that clearly telegraphed, *Get the hell away from me.*

There were a few other women and a couple of men

standing around on the sidewalk in front of the abandoned stores. One of the women, dressed in a tight red miniskirt and stiletto heels, waved at the driver Glo had just rebuffed. He put his car in reverse and backed toward her.

Christy bit her lip. This abandoned shopping center was a hangout for hookers. She debated whether to stop the car and get out to talk to Glo, or to invite Glo into the car. She finally decided it would be safer for both of them if Glo got into the car.

After glancing around to make sure there was no one else hovering nearby, Christy pulled up in front of the shaded entrance to the drug store and rolled down the passenger side window. Glo looked up from under her brows. Christy waved and called her name.

Glo's face shone with relief. She climbed in on the passenger side, bringing with her the smell of stale cigarettes and a chill that didn't match the temperature outside. She huddled in the seat just as she'd huddled against the building, her shoulders hunched, her arms crossed, her head down.

Christy drove. "That looks like a dangerous place to hang out."

"Yeah." Glo's voice sounded scornful, as if she were thinking, *Like you'd know anything about it.*

"What did you have to tell me?"

"You've got the—you know—the money?"

"Yes, when you tell me what you know." Christy assessed Glo out of the corner of her eye. The girl seemed harmless, especially as compared to her brother Jazzy, but Christy was fully aware that she could be hiding a knife or a gun in those folded arms.

A pang of fear dug into her chest, joining the apprehension that had taken up residence there the day she'd gotten the call about her father's arrest. Had she made a mistake letting Glo into the car?

As if she'd heard Christy's silent question, Glo pressed her lips together, closed her eyes and shook her head. Her shoulders straightened slightly. "I heard Jazzy talking on the phone last night. He was really upset. I could hear him yelling, telling somebody they better hope Buddy wasn't under arrest, because he owed Jazzy some stuff."

"Buddy?" Christy said. "Buddy Kramer?"

"That's the only Buddy I know. I called a girlfriend who dates him. He was picked up by the police down at the Hotel Winsor—you know—where I told you he hung out? My girlfriend said it was something about a gun. She said that was all she knew."

"I already know that, Glo. He was picked up because his fingerprint was found on a shell casing from—from a shooting."

"Oh." Glo hunched down again. She mumbled something.

"What? I didn't hear you."

"I can't help it if you already heard that. You said you'd give me some money."

"I said I would if you had information for me. Something I don't already know."

Glo was silent for a few moments. Then she pulled a battered pack of cigarettes out of a pocket.

"You can't smoke in the car." Christy hated cigarette smoke, but that wasn't the only reason she objected. Maybe the need for a cigarette would spur Glo into revealing what else she knew. The faster Glo could get her money, the faster she could get out of the car and have her smoke.

Christy was sure Glo knew more than she'd told so far. She seemed to be struggling with the question of how much to share. Or maybe she was afraid.

"Who was Jazzy talking to about Buddy?"

"I told you, I don't know."

"Come on, Glo. Jazzy's your brother, right? You live with him. I doubt you're totally oblivious to what he does."

Glo didn't answer.

After a couple of minutes, as Christy made a turn and headed back in the direction of the abandoned drug store, Glo sat up.

"Okay. I do know something. But he'll kill me if he finds out I told."

"Who'll kill you? Jazzy?"

"Uh, yeah."

The tentative reply meant Jazzy wasn't the only one Glo was afraid of.

"Listen to me, Glo. I'm trying to find out who killed my sister. Anything you tell me is going to help me do that. So why would I rat on you?" Christy said solemnly, a little surprised at herself for using the word *rat*. "You're the one who's helping me."

"What I know's worth a lot more than a hundred bucks."

Christy pulled over to the side of the road and stopped the car. "That's it, Glo. Get out," she said calmly.

"What?"

"Get out. I'm happy to give you more money, but I don't have unlimited funds, and I'm beginning to think all you're doing is extorting me."

"Extorting? You mean like blackmail?"

"No, like trying to get money for nothing. So go on. Get out of the car." Christy's heart was pounding. She was treading on dangerous ground. She had no idea if Glo had a weapon. In fact, she wasn't sure that she could hold her own in a fight, weapon or no. Her wrist was still impaired and she wasn't desperate. Glo was. She held her breath and waited to see if her bluff had worked.

Glo studied her face for a long time. She seemed to be having an internal argument with herself. Within a few moments, her eyes filled with tears and she wiped her nose with the back of her hand.

"This is probably going to get me killed, or put in prison," Glo finally said in a choked voice. "But it's tearing me apart. I can't stand it anymore."

Christy waited, forcing herself to breathe normally.

"Jazzy—" Glo stopped and swallowed. "Jazzy and Buddy, they got a deal working—with some cops. They rat on people—you know—sometimes it's druggies, sometimes it's about a killing or something. In return the cops give them drugs."

Christy's heart leaped with excitement. "Drugs? From a policeman?" she said, not even having to feign shock. It didn't matter that she already knew there were drugs from police evidence on the streets. It still was a stunning revelation to hear it confirmed.

"I don't know how it works, but I've seen some of the drugs. They're marked—you know—like stuff the cops already took in a raid or something."

"Who are the cops, Glo?"

"Oh, no. No, no, no. You don't understand. I don't know who they are. I don't!"

Was Glo protesting too much? Or was she just afraid that without the police officers' names Christy wouldn't give her the money?

"I think you do," Christy said, trying to keep her voice strong and steady.

"No, really." Glo shook her head vehemently. "All I did was see some of the stuff. Jazzy had some and—and so did Autumn."

That surprised Christy. "Autumn? Glo, please tell me you're not talking about five years ago."

"No! I mean—you know—the stuff Autumn had, yeah.

But here's the deal. She told me her boyfriend had given it to her. Said it came from the police station."

"But you've seen some since, right?"

Glo reached for her cigarettes then checked herself. "Yeah. I told you. But don't ask me who the cops are. All I know is Jazzy and Buddy got a deal going with 'em."

Ahead, Christy saw the shopping center. She turned into the parking lot and surveyed the storefronts. Her eye was caught by a familiar scarecrow-thin figure lurking in a dark alley between stores. "Was there anyone with you?"

"What?"

"Is that Jazzy? In that alley?" Christy pointed.

Glo looked and gasped. "Oh, no. He can't know I'm talking to you."

Christy realized Jazzy was talking to someone who stood farther back in the shadows. "Who's that with him?" she asked.

Glo craned her neck. "Oh, no—" she breathed. "It's—his cop friend."

Christy squinted, but she couldn't make out the cop's features. The alley was too dark. "I thought you didn't know the cop."

"I don't know his name, but I've seen him a few times. He's a big guy. Usually wears a suit."

A suit. That meant he was a detective. Was it Autumn's boyfriend? She wanted to get closer, get a better look. She eased the car forward.

"What are you doing?" Glo exclaimed. "Don't go any closer. If they see me in the car with you, I'm dead!"

Christy pulled into a parking place, out in the open. She didn't cut the engine, just sat with her foot on the brake. "Glo, I need to know who the policeman is. I need you to find out."

Glo recoiled and her pale face grew whiter. "I can't do that.

I don't ask Jazzy nothing. I keep quiet and he gives me—"
She ducked her head. "He gives me drugs. He'd throw me
out if I started asking questions."

"Glo, I have to know something about the police officer.
Anything. It's very, very important."

"I told you, I—"

"Listen to me, Glo. He may have killed Autumn. Your
friend. My sister. Now I know she told you something about
him. Anything, no matter how small." Christy felt tears well
in her eyes. She put her hand on Glo's thin arm. "Please."

Glo pressed her lips together and squeezed her eyes shut
again. "I'm scared," she whispered.

"I know. Listen, I promise you, when all this is over, I'll
help you. If you'd like to try to get clean, I'll help you. I'd
have done it for Autumn, but I never got the chance. Since I
couldn't help her, I'd like to help you. Would you want to do
that?"

Glo looked up at her, eyes shining with tears. "I tried once,
but it was too hard. I couldn't afford to live on my own, and
Jazzy just kept on using."

"I'll help you get into a program. Please, Glo?"

Glo took a deep shaky breath. "I think Autumn's boyfriend
was Jazzy's cop. That guy we just saw. She told me he was a
big shot—you know, a detective."

Christy's heart leaped. She was right. "A detective? Here
in St. Tammany Parish? Or down in New Orleans?"

Glo shrugged. "I think here, but I don't know. She wouldn't
say. She was—you know, proud that he trusted her to keep his
secret. She called him some nickname, but I can't remember
what it was."

A detective.

"Thank you. That helps." Christy reached into her pocket
and pulled out the twenties. "Here. If you think of anything

else—his nickname—anything, call me. And don't forget about my offer."

Glo stuffed the money into the pocket of her ragged jeans, then craned her neck to look back toward the narrow alley where her brother had been standing.

Christy followed her gaze. The alley was empty. Jazzy and his cop friend were gone. "Looks like they're gone now."

"I—don't want to get out here. Can you take me back to the house?"

Christy reluctantly agreed.

Within fifteen minutes, they were at Glo's house. Christy pulled up in front of the door, and Glo immediately moved to get out.

"Don't forget, Glo. When this is all over, I'll get you into rehab. Okay?"

Glo sent Christy a searching look. "Sure," she said, an ironic tone in her voice. "If we're both still alive."

Reilly breathed a little easier as the thin, drug-ravaged young woman climbed out of Christy's rental car in front of a ramshackle house on Salvation Road.

"Damn it, Christy," he muttered. "The worst street in the worst part of Chef Voleur."

Still, within just a few moments, she'd be out of there and safe.

The past hour had felt like the longest sixty minutes of his life. But Christy had made it so far without getting herself hurt. Which to Reilly's mind was a miracle.

He'd followed her to the rental car place, then to the hospital. While she was visiting her father, he'd gotten Dawson's state-of-the-art GPS tracker positioned under her rental car.

Sure enough, when Christy left the hospital, she didn't turn toward his condo. She headed straight for the roughest section of Chef Voleur, where abandoned buildings had been turned into crack houses and whorehouses. When he realized where she was going, he'd very nearly called a police cruiser to stop her.

Instead, when she'd turned into the parking lot of an abandoned strip mall, he'd crept as close as he dared, and left his car in gear.

It had been hell to watch her drive up to one of the hookers loitering in the shadows and talk to her. Hell to do nothing when the girl got into her car. Hell to watch them drive off. If the girl had a weapon and decided to use it, Christy wouldn't have a chance. He'd never be able to get to her in time.

Now he rubbed the day's growth of beard on his cheeks and jaw and wished he'd done what he'd been threatening to do from the beginning—lock Christy up as a material witness and force her to talk.

Material witness to what? He scoffed. He wasn't on an official case, and he had no proof that she was holding anything the police could use. So here he was, working off the clock, with little more authority than a private detective.

With her hand on the door handle, the girl ducked her head back into the car's interior to say something to Christy. Reilly studied her. Who was she? How had Christy found her? And what was her connection to Autumn?

He knew there was one. The only reason Christy would come down to this part of town was to get information about her sister.

Just about the time the girl straightened and went to close the car door, the door to the house behind her opened and a thin, tattooed clone of Tommy Lee came out, gesturing wildly and yelling at her. Reilly couldn't make out what he was saying.

Behind him, silhouetted in the dark doorway, Reilly saw another figure. One that looked familiar.

"What the hell?" he whispered as he studied the broad,

high forehead and arrogant stance. He squinted, having trouble believing his eyes.

Was that really Dagewood, the obnoxious detective who worked with Ryker? The guy cocked his head, glancing at the vehicles parked on the street and giving Reilly a clearer look at his face. There was no mistaking those broad features. It definitely was Dagewood.

The tattooed guy must be Dagewood's CI.

Reilly hunched down in his seat, hoping the detective couldn't see him, and grabbed his handgun from the glove compartment. He debated whether to leave his engine running or kill it.

The Tommy Lee clone grabbed the girl by the arm and jerked her away from Christy's open passenger door. He snatched what looked like folded money out of her hand, then shoved her roughly to the ground.

Reilly ejected and checked the gun's magazine, then reinserted it.

This situation could get ugly—fast.

Get out of here, Christy.

CHRISTY WATCHED IN HORROR as Jazzy grabbed the twenties out of Glo's hand and roughly shoved her to the ground. She jumped out of the car and yelled across the roof. "Hey! Jazzy! Stop that. Glo! Get back in the car."

Glo jumped up, glanced toward Christy, then turned and swung her fist at Jazzy. "Gimme my money!" she shouted.

Jazzy stopped Glo's swing by grabbing her wrist. He twisted it and pushed her down again. She hit the ground, rolled and scrambled up.

"Glo! Come on. Let's get out of here," Christy called, but Glo ran toward the house, still screaming at Jazzy.

Beyond Glo, Christy saw a big man step out from the darkened doorway as Glo shot past him and into the house.

He was in dress pants and a long-sleeved shirt, a huge contrast to Jazzy's threadbare T-shirt and tattered jeans.

The man's gaze met hers, hostility and fury in his eyes. Then he turned to Jazzy. "Get her!" he shouted.

She tried to jump back into the car and close the door, but Jazzy was surprisingly fast, belying his malnourished, over-medicated appearance.

He was around the front of the car before she got her foot inside. Grabbing her hair, he dragged her out and wrapped his bony arms around her in a bear hug. He was surprisingly strong for such a skinny guy.

Christy struggled. She tried to kick, bite, scratch—anything to make Jazzy let go of her. She sucked in air to scream, almost gagging at the sour stench of cigarettes, beer and body odor, but Jazzy's arms were too tight around her chest. All she could manage was a weak squeal.

Just as Jazzy dragged her over the concrete stoop, she heard a shout.

"Stop! Police! Let her go."

She knew that voice! Reilly! She twisted, looking for him but Jazzy jerked her back around.

Christy struggled with all her might. If she let Jazzy get her inside, there was no telling what would happen to her. She screamed again. It was barely louder than her first try.

"Let. Her. Go!" Reilly yelled.

Jazzy let loose a string of inventive curse words. He took his left arm from its death grip around her and grabbed a handful of her hair again. Furious, impotent tears sprang to her eyes and she reached up, hoping to pry loose his grip.

"Stop! Dagewood, stop him!" Reilly yelled.

Suddenly, a gun appeared in the big man's hand. He raised it, aiming, not at Jazzy, but in the direction of Reilly's voice.

"No!" she cried. "Reilly!"

The man took aim and fired a shot in Reilly's direction.

"No!" Christy screamed again, just as Jazzy shoved her through the open doorway. She stumbled and fell against a table. Fireworks exploded in her head, then everything went black.

Chapter Fourteen

Reilly cringed without breaking stride as the slug whizzed past his head.

Son of a bitch! Dagewood was shooting at him. He must not recognize him.

Reilly had broken into a run as soon as Tommy Lee Clone had started toward Christy, but he'd still been fifty feet away when the guy shoved her forcefully through the doorway.

"Dagewood! It's Reilly Delancey!" he shouted.

To Reilly's shock, Dagewood took slow, careful aim and fired another round at him. Then he calmly stepped backward, through the doorway, and slammed the door.

In a few strides Reilly slammed into the door at full speed. It didn't break. His momentum bounced him backward and he nearly lost his footing. His chest heaved painfully as his lungs struggled for oxygen.

He aimed his weapon at the door's lock. But he couldn't shoot. Not blindly like that. Christy was in there.

From the other side of the door, a report split the air and a bullet plowed through the wood of the door. It hit the ground a few feet behind Reilly.

He had no choice but to retreat behind Christy's rental car. He fished his cell phone out of his pocket, cursing. He should have called for backup when he first saw what was going on.

But he hadn't realized that Dagewood was the enemy. Up until the instant Dagewood had aimed his gun at him, Reilly had still expected the detective to stop Tommy Lee.

He speed-dialed the SWAT commander, absently noticing doors easing open up and down the street, and curtains fluttering at darkened windows. *Stay in your houses,* he silently begged the onlookers as Ace came on the line.

"Commander Acer. Delancey here. I've got a situation—" Reilly glanced at a bent street sign. "I'm at the corner of Salvation and Fortune. Need backup. ASAP."

"What's the situation?" Ace asked. Typically, he wasted no time on useless questions.

"I'm outside a house where one female, possibly two, are being held hostage by a white male in his mid- to late-twenties and—a police detective named Dagewood."

Uncharacteristically, there was silence on the other end of the phone. "Repeat?" Ace barked.

"Detective Dagewood," Reilly stated clearly. "Don't know his first name. He fired at me before going into the house with the white male and the hostages."

"Delancey, are you sure about this?" Reilly couldn't blame Ace for the question. He'd seen Dagewood aim at him, felt and heard the whoosh of air as Dagewood's bullet barely missed him and he still had trouble believing it. "Yes, sir," he replied.

"Do not try to enter the house, Delancey. That's an order."

"Yes, sir."

"Sending team now. 10-4."

Damn Ace for issuing that order. Reilly wanted another chance at the door. This time he'd use his foot, putting all his weight behind the kick rather than ramming it with his shoulder. But Ace had given him an order, and he was bound to honor it. He prayed the team would get there soon.

"Dagewood!" he yelled at the door. "What's going on?"

No answer except another bullet fired through the door.

"Dagewood!"

He heard scuffling from inside. He hoped to hell they weren't escaping through the back door. He couldn't risk leaving his position to check.

Come on, Ace.

Three doors down, an elderly man stepped out into his yard and shaded his eyes with one hand. Reilly gestured for him to go back inside.

The man yelled something that Reilly didn't catch, then hurried back toward his door.

Breathing a sigh of relief, Reilly went to pocket his phone, then paused. Ryker would have Dagewood's cell number. He called him. "I need Detective Dagewood's cell," he said.

"Reilly? What—? What's going on?"

"Dagewood's holding Christy hostage in a drug house."

"He's—? I don't— Are you sure?"

"Yes."

Ryker muttered a curse. "Hang on. Let me get my cell." Reilly heard him moving about.

"Okay, here it is."

Reilly punched the numbers into his phone after Ryker read them. Then his brother asked, "Where are you, kid?"

"Can't talk. SWAT's on the way."

"Reilly—"

Reilly cut the connection and called Dagewood. The phone rang so long he decided that the detective didn't have it with him or wasn't going to answer. Finally, he heard a click. He waited, but Dagewood didn't speak.

"Dagewood, this is Reilly Delancey."

Still nothing.

"We need to talk," he said in his best hostage-negotiator

tone. "Send Christy and the other woman out, and then you and I can discuss this."

"Go to hell," Dagewood said and hung up.

Reilly called back.

Dagewood didn't answer.

Reilly kept trying though. Three times. He let the phone ring until voice mail picked up, then hung up and called again.

Then he tried Christy's number. He heard it ring—from inside the rental car. He opened the driver's side door. There on the floorboard, was Christy's purse.

He picked it up and dumped it onto the seat. He saw her cell phone—and a second phone. That must be the one he'd heard ring in her room. The one she'd lied about, telling him she'd changed her ring tone.

He picked it up and paged through the contacts. *Triple A, Dr. Adams, D.B., Caesar's Pizza, Christy, Dad, Frankie, Glo, Jazzy, Laurie, Super D.*

It was Autumn's phone! It had to be. *Laurie* had to be Laurie Kestler, Autumn's high school friend that Christy had mentioned.

Reilly reviewed the names again, stopping at Glo. Hadn't Tommy Lee called the girl Glo? So who was he? *D.B.? Frankie? Jazzy?*

He viewed each number. When he came to the listing for D.B., he did a double take. He checked the number Ryker had just given him. Sure enough, it was Dagewood's cell phone. D.B was Detective Dagewood.

The terrible realization that had been growing inside him for days now blossomed into certainty. Autumn's boyfriend was a cop—a detective. *Dagewood* had given Christy's sister the marked drugs.

Did that mean Dagewood had killed Christy's sister?

Quickly, keeping one eye out for any movement from inside

the house, Reilly rummaged through the rest of the contents of Christy's purse. He'd bet a year's pay that somewhere in here was evidence implicating Dagewood. The evidence Christy had been hiding from him.

He searched through her wallet. In the bill compartment, he found two pieces of folded paper.

As he pulled out the first one, he heard engines, big engines. From up the street he saw the big, black SUVs of the SWAT team approaching. Behind them were four police cars. Two of the cars maneuvered into the crossways of the street at either end of the block, forming a blockade. The SUVs pulled up behind them.

With the sound of all the vehicles, more onlookers opened their doors and ventured out onto the street. When they saw the police cars and uniformed officers, they scurried back inside their houses.

Reilly kept one eye on the activity as he unfolded the piece of lined paper and read the note. "Hey. Meet me at the shack. I'm 10-10 at 12. Got some stuff for you. B."

10-10 was police code for off duty. Reilly's heart sank to his toes. So this was what Christy had been hiding from him. She'd been holding evidence all this time that Autumn's boyfriend was a cop. He thought about her mother dying from a policeman's bullet, and her refusal to trust him. A strange mixture of anger and understanding swelled in his chest.

Damn it, Christy. Why didn't she believe that he was one of the good guys? He'd failed her and he didn't even know how.

He turned his full attention back to the note. Had Dagewood written it? He frowned. The letter *B* didn't mean anything to him. Particularly frustrating, since "D.B." was also how Autumn had listed Dagewood's number in her phone.

He stuck the note in his pocket and pulled out the other piece of paper. It was wrapped around a disk. Reilly unwrapped it. A brass button, the same design as the sheriff's department dress uniforms. Not that the button was that unique, but given the other evidence...

Granted, it was circumstantial. Still, the body of evidence left little room for doubt. Dagewood was definitely a prime suspect in Autumn Moser's death.

Out of the corner of his eye, Reilly saw movement in the direction of the blockade. He looked up. Commander Acer was coming his way, dressed in body armor and carrying a sniper rifle.

Reilly met him halfway.

"Situation?" Ace asked.

Reilly pointed. "Detective Dagewood, the younger male, a female named Glo and Christy Moser are inside. I'm in possession of evidence gathered by Christy Moser that implicates Dagewood in the death of Christy's sister."

Ace's dark eyes searched Reilly's face. Then he nodded. "Back entrance?"

Reilly shook his head. "Unknown."

Ace spoke into the microphone attached to the left shoulder of his uniform as he pointed at the house. "Two cars, cover the back door."

"I'm going back up there. I'm going to try to talk my way in," Reilly said.

Ace shook his head. "I'll handle it," he said. "You're too close to the situation."

Reilly's stomach sank. He shook his head. "Sir, I need to do this. I promised Christy I'd keep her safe."

Ace studied Reilly's face for a few seconds. Reilly expected him to order him back to the blockade. "I'll take the back then."

"Dagewood fired at me twice, and has fired through the front door several times. I don't know if the other guy has a gun." Reilly took a breath. "And I don't know the condition of the women."

Ace nodded, his face grim. "10-4," he said.

Reilly glanced at the other SWAT team members. They were dressed in their uniforms with body armor and helmets. One of them held up a vest and gestured at Reilly.

Reilly nodded, so the officer heaved the vest toward him. He caught it and quickly put it on. The same officer held up a helmet. Reilly started to hold up his hands to catch it, then decided against it.

With a helmet on, Christy might not recognize him. Once he got inside, he needed her to know it was him. He needed her to know she could trust him.

He shook his head, declining the helmet, then held his hand up to the side of his head, thumb and pinkie finger spread, the other three bent, mimicking a telephone handset. The helmets were wired, so if he went in without one, he'd need a way to communicate with the rest of the team.

The officer quickly retrieved a wireless headset and tossed it. Reilly put it on. Now he'd be able to hear the SWAT team members and they could hear him.

He headed back down the street and positioned himself behind the rental car again. Then he called Dagewood.

After a long time, Dagewood answered, again without speaking.

"What are you doing, Dagewood? What do you want?"

"I want you to address me by my title!"

Reilly let out his breath in a whoosh. Finally, the detective was talking. "Yes, sir, Detective. I'm happy to do that. Can you tell me what you want, Detective Dagewood?"

Silence. Then Dagewood said, "I want you to leave. I've got business to attend to in here, and I can't get it done with you bothering me. Don't think I'm fooled by your psychobabble negotiator talk."

"I don't think that, sir."

"Tell your SWAT buddies out there to leave too. I've got this situation under control. I'm in charge here. I'll call for backup if I need it."

Reilly knew from the tone of Dagewood's voice that he was highly stressed. On the verge of panic. His tone was pitched high, his voice brittle and tight. Dagewood was a bomb about to explode.

Ace's voice came through the headset. "Keep him talking, Reilly. We're going to try to get a shot from the back."

Reilly's pulse hammered. His SWAT teammates were the best, but he didn't want sniper bullets anywhere near Christy.

"Okay," he said carefully, hoping his words made sense to Ace as well as to Dagewood. "I'm glad you've got everything under control. Is everybody inside doing okay? Any injuries?"

Reilly changed his tone from the obsequious tone of earlier. Now he spoke to Dagewood as if he were a fellow officer who happened to be on the inside, rather than the enemy. He hoped it would put the detective at ease.

"Everyone's fine, so far," Dagewood bit out. "But they won't be if you don't get the SWAT team off my back. I've just got a little business to attend to."

"Can I help you with that?" Reilly asked, as casually as he could.

"I don't need help from a traffic cop. I'm a detective."

"Yes, sir," Reilly said. "Just thought I could lend a hand." He paused for a second. "Can you tell me what you need Christy for?"

No answer.

"Do you know who Christy is, Detective?"

"Yeah." The answer was quiet. "She's Moser's daughter."

Out of the corner of his eye, Reilly saw the SWAT team

approaching in formation, crouched behind the big metal shields, as per protocol. Hal Carter, a buddy of his, signaled to him that Ace was in place in the back. Reilly nodded.

"That's right. The serial killer." Reilly took a breath and asked casually, "You knew her sister, didn't you?"

"Cut that tone, boy," Dagewood yelled, "or *Christy* is going to be missing some necessary parts."

"Yes, sir," Reilly answered earnestly. *God, don't let him hurt her.* "Listen, Detective, why don't you let me inside? Christy can come out, and I'll come in. Even trade."

"What the *hell* do I want you for?"

The SWAT team was getting closer. Reilly held up his hand. The team leader shook his head. Reilly stared at him and held up his hand again. Reluctantly, the leader nodded and gestured to the team to halt.

"I'd like to come in, Detective. I'd like to understand what's going on. Maybe I can help."

"Do not enter the house," Ace's voice boomed in his ear. "That's an order."

Reilly winced. If he could talk his way in, he would, orders or not. He had to save Christy.

"Reilly!" It was Christy's voice, faint, terrified, coming through the phone. He almost crumpled in relief. She was okay, at least okay enough to talk.

Then he heard a smack. "Shut up!" The tattooed guy had hit her.

Reilly growled under his breath.

Dagewood muttered something Reilly couldn't catch.

"Detective Dagewood, I don't know what you want in order to let Christy go, but I'm willing to work with you. Come on. Open the door. I'm not armed. All I want to do is try and end this as peacefully as possible."

"End it? You don't know—" Dagewood's voice cut out.

"Detective?"

"Let him in," he heard Dagewood say in an aside, then, "You make one false move, Delancey, and your girlfriend here goes down with a bullet in the brain. Got it?"

Reilly glanced at Hal, who was leading the SWAT team. He held up his gun, then laid it on top of the car.

"Reilly, don't be an idiot," Hal said softly through the headset, but Reilly ignored him.

He rounded the front of the car and walked up to the door. Just as he stepped up onto the stoop he heard a click. He reached out and twisted the knob, hoping he wasn't about to open the door to his death.

He pushed the door open. The interior was dark. Hell, compared with the sunny world outside, it was black as pitch. The door slammed behind him.

At the same time he heard Christy's panicked voice. "Reilly—no!"

He instinctively ducked, but he was too late. Searing heat exploded inside him, slamming him back against the door. He crumpled. The fire spread, until it engulfed his whole body.

"Jazzy, check him. See if he reacts." That was Dagewood.

A hard shoe rammed him in the side—twice. He arched in pain and groaned. He couldn't see, couldn't think. Another blow. He gasped, then growled.

"You're alive," Dagewood said. "Too bad."

Reilly tried to move. Hot pain shot through his left shoulder. He *was* alive. No dead person could hurt this much.

Then Christy screamed. "No!"

Reilly squinted. He could barely make out Dagewood's silhouette, holding a handgun pointed right at him.

"Detective," Reilly rasped, holding up a hand. "You've got me. You can shoot me, let Tommy Lee here stomp me—" he took a ragged breath "—whatever. Just—let Christy and—and Glo go."

The tattooed guy kicked his left shoulder. A white-hot grenade exploded behind Reilly's eyelids. He shrieked.

"Please stop!" Christy begged.

"Jazzy, back off," Dagewood ordered.

Jazzy. The name penetrated the haze still obscuring Reilly's brain. Dagewood had said the name earlier. And it was one of the names in Autumn's phone.

"So, Delancey who didn't make detective, what the hell are you trying to do? Get me out of the way so you can take my job?"

Doing his best to ignore the pain in the left side of his chest and the warm blood that was flowing out to soak his shoulder and his shirt, Reilly pushed himself into a sitting position. He replayed Dagewood's words in his head. "Take your job?" he rasped. "I don't know—what you're talking about."

"Yeah?" Dagewood still had his gun pointed at Reilly's chest. "Maybe this will help you figure it out." He pulled the trigger.

Reilly yelped in pain as the bullet slammed square into the center of his chest.

From far away, he heard screaming.

Reilly struggled for air. The body armor had stopped the bullet from penetrating his skin, he realized. But the impact had stung like a hornet and thrown his lungs into spasm. He gasped.

"Reilly!" Christy cried.

Through the haze of pain that engulfed him, he made out Ace's voice in his ears.

Move in. Move in. Shots fired. Hold ready at fifty feet.

Dagewood cocked his head. "See! You've got SWAT here

and you're still trying to tell me you didn't plan this to get rid of me and take my detective slot?"

Reilly shook his head, still struggling to breathe. He had no idea what Dagewood was talking about.

"You'd better tell your SWAT buddies to back off or I'll shoot you where there's no body armor."

"Commander—stand down," he rasped. "Stand—down."

"10-4," Ace said. "You tell the bastard I said 10-4."

Reilly nodded. "The commander said 10-4," he said to Dagewood.

Reilly squeezed his eyes shut, fighting to clear his head. Why was Dagewood raving about his detective position? Ever since Ryker had made detective, Dagewood, egged on by his buddy Phillips, had delighted in digging at Reilly about not being chosen. But what did that have to do with Christy's quest to find her sister's murderer?

"Reilly didn't know what I was doing," Christy cried. "I'm the one who figured out that it was you who was supplying drugs to Autumn. Reilly had no idea."

Dagewood turned on Christy. "You shut the hell up!" he barked. "You played right into his hands. He's always wanted my job. Damn Delanceys. They always get what they want."

Reilly's brain was becoming less hazy, and he was beginning to piece together the evidence. The telephone number labeled D.B., the note, the bag of drugs and the brass button.

Even the gun. Reilly's chest ached and he still felt like he couldn't get a full breath, but he had to get Dagewood's attention off Christy and back onto him. "The gun," he said hoarsely.

Dagewood's head snapped around.

Something was tickling his left arm. He looked down. The sticky redness was spreading down his arm. He forced his brain to concentrate on what he was trying to tell Dagewood.

"The gun that killed Autumn Moser. It was your throw-away, wasn't it? You got it from Kramer."

Dagewood's broad face turned bright red. "Shut up," he muttered. "Just shut up."

"Why didn't you get rid of it after you shot Autumn?"

He heard Christy gasp.

Dagewood lifted the barrel of his gun until it was pointed at Reilly's head. "You'd better shut the hell up."

"It was Kramer's fault, wasn't it? You told him to get rid of it, but he didn't. So did Kramer shoot at Christy? Or was that you?"

"Hah," Jazzy said from the other side of the room, where he was pacing back and forth and sweating, obviously in need of a fix. "That's how much you know," he slurred. "I shot—"

"You idiot!" Dagcwood shouted and aimed at Jazzy.

"You killed my sister!" Christy shouted. "She screamed 'Bum'! That was you! Of course!"

Reilly couldn't make sense of what she'd said. Who was Bum?

"That's what Autumn was screaming just before the gun-shots. 'No, Bum.' It was you—!" Christy's voice broke.

Dagewood took a step backward. Reilly tensed. That with-drawal meant one of two things. He was stepping away to aim at Christy, or he was feeling cornered—or both. Either way, it wasn't a good sign.

"Bum! Dagewood!" Her voice went higher with excite-ment. "Like Dagwood Bumstead!"

In his ear, Reilly heard Ace's voice again. "Team, is there a resolution?"

And the answer, from one of the snipers. "I've got a resolution."

Reilly knew the term *resolution* meant he had a clear shot.

Dagewood turned the gun on Christy again. "She wanted out. We had a good thing and she wanted out. She was going to ruin everything."

"Dagewood," Reilly said quickly. "Why don't—"

"You shut up!" he shouted at Reilly, then turned back to Christy. "She had to talk to you when you called. I *told* her not to answer the phone. I *warned* her. You heard everything, didn't you? Why'd you have to come back here and stir things up?"

Christy shook her head.

"Don't lie to me!"

"Dagewood," Reilly broke in. His head was spinning from trying to concentrate on their words while the burning in his shoulder fanned itself into an inferno. "Why don't you give me the gun? You know how this is going to go down if you don't. Come on. We can walk out of here."

"No! Shut up!" Dagewood took another step backward. "I'm a *detective*. That's what I am. I can't give that up." He gave a kind of half sob. Then his gun hand wavered.

Reilly's heart sped up. That waver—was he considering dropping the gun? Carefully, slowly, Reilly gathered every bit of strength he had and began to push himself to his feet. His shoe slipped in blood that had dripped from his arm onto the floor, but he managed to get his feet under him.

Dagewood's dark eyes snapped Reilly's way.

"Everything will work out now," Reilly said, using pre-arranged phrases designed to calm the hostage taker while communicating with the SWAT team.

He heard Ace's voice in his ear. "Hold on the resolution. Repeat—hold."

Dagewood nodded. Sweat poured down his red face and dripped from his chin. He crooked his elbow, pointing the gun's barrel at the ceiling. Another good sign.

"Okay," Reilly said. "Let's talk about how we're going to get out of here."

Dagewood's eyes were wide and unblinking. Reilly could see white all the way around the irises.

"What do you say, Detective? Can we let the women go now?"

Dagewood nodded again. The bright flush was leaving his face.

Reilly's legs were trembling and he could feel more blood flowing down to his elbow and dripping off, but he finally managed to stand. Oddly, his shoulder had stopped burning. Or his whole body was burning at the same temperature. He wasn't sure which.

He blinked. He couldn't quite read Dagewood. The man's gun hand was trembling, he swayed on his feet and his florid cheeks and neck were losing color at an alarming rate.

"I'm going to tell Christy and Glo to get up off the couch now, okay?"

The detective's fingers tightened around the grip of the gun.

Reilly held up a hand, signaling Christy and Glo to stay still for the moment. "What do you say?"

"I'm a *detective*," Dagewood repeated.

Reilly saw the man's fingertips turn white. He took a step toward him. "That's right, Detective—" he said softly. "Everything's going to work out—"

In a deliberate, unhurried motion, Dagewood pressed the tip of the barrel against his head.

"No!" Reilly screamed and sprang forward with all the strength he had left in him, but his voice was drowned out by the gun blast.

Through a red-spotted haze he saw Christy and Glo's mouths open, but if they were screaming, he couldn't tell.

Then the room was swarming with black-garbed officers in body armor and helmets and guns.

The last thing he heard was Ace's solemn, regretful voice in his ear. "We were damn unlucky this time."

Chapter Fifteen

Before the echo of the gunshot had faded, before Christy had fully processed what had happened, the shabby room in the ramshackle house was overrun with men in black uniforms with helmets, shields and guns.

Dazed and in shock from the awful sight of Detective Dagewood shooting himself, she hardly remembered what had happened next. She vaguely remembered being guided out of the house to a waiting ambulance, which sped off to the St. Tammany Parish hospital while EMTs cleaned the blood and brain matter off her and checked to be sure she was uninjured.

She asked everyone she saw, EMTs, physicians, nurses, clerical staff, about Reilly, but she didn't get an answer until Detective Ryker Delancey came into the emergency room cubicle where the ER nursing supervisor had deposited her and told her to stay put.

"Detective Delancey," she said, recognizing him immediately as Reilly's brother. How she'd ever thought the two of them looked alike, she didn't know. Reilly was much more handsome, and less somber. His eyes were bluer too, she was sure.

"How is Reilly?" she asked. "Please tell me he's okay."

"They've got him in surgery to remove the bullet from his

shoulder. It nicked the bone, so the surgery may take a while. But they tell me he's doing fine."

"What about the other shot. That—Dagewood shot him in the chest. I thought Reilly was dead!"

Ryker nodded. "His body armor stopped the bullet. He's going to have a monstrous bruise, and they think the impact may have broken a rib, but he was lucky."

She nodded, feeling very close to tears. "It was my fault. If I hadn't gone down there to talk to Glo, this wouldn't have happened."

"Blaming yourself isn't going to solve anything," Ryker said in his direct, pragmatic way. "It would have all come to a head eventually. Reilly knew the danger."

She cleared her throat and tried to swallow the knot that had lodged there. "I can't stop thinking about him, bleeding and hurt. Yet he still tried—to stop Dagewood from shooting himself."

Ryker nodded. "The ER has released you. I'm going to take you out to the waiting room. My fiancée Nicole is there. She's going to drive you back to Reilly's place so you can get some sleep. I'll stay here until he's out of surgery."

Christy started to protest that she wanted to stay too, but the visions in her head stopped her. Visions of Detective Dagewood shooting Reilly—a fellow police officer. The house swarming with SWAT officers dressed like—like ninjas or special ops soldiers or something.

And Reilly, hurt and bleeding, because of her. Because she'd refused to trust him enough to tell him the whole truth.

She just needed to get away—from the police, from the hospital, from everything. At least for a little while. Guilt washed over her as she thought about her father, lying upstairs in the cardiac care unit, critically ill. But no matter how selfish it was, she didn't even want to see him right now. She needed some time alone.

Ryker led her out to the waiting room and introduced her to Nicole Beckham, his fiancée. Nicole was a pixielike young woman with a personality as pert as her appearance. When she saw Christy though, she gave one searching look into her eyes and said, "Come on. Let's get you home. You look like you need some alone time."

Dazedly, Christy reflected that she'd probably love to have Nicole as a friend, later, when and if she was able to crawl out of this numbing mental fog.

She waited until she and Nicole were alone in Nicole's car to tell her she didn't want to stay at Reilly's. She preferred to go to a hotel.

HER FATHER WAS DEAD. Christy had gotten the call in the middle of her meeting with the chief of staff at Children's Hospital in Boston. With permission from the St. Tammany Parish sheriff's office, she'd flown back there to make arrangements for a leave of absence to care for her dad. But he'd gone into cardiac arrest less than forty-eight hours after she'd boarded the plane.

Now she stood under the canopy at the Shady Lawn Cemetery in Covington, as a slow, cold rain fell. It soaked into her shoes and seeped through her coat and into her very bones. There was nothing more miserable than a cold rain in Louisiana.

She watched the cemetery workers operate the mechanical device that lowered her dad's coffin into the ground between her mother and sister. The funeral director had tried to get her to leave, but she wasn't ready. She wanted some time by herself, to say goodbye to her family.

Getting that time alone hadn't been easy. To her surprise, there had been reporters and curious onlookers at the funeral and at the grave site. She'd been escorted through the crowd by the funeral director, who had shielded her under a huge black umbrella. Then the hired pallbearers had clustered around her, hiding her from the rubberneckers and the TV cameras, while two policemen politely but firmly refused to allow anyone to get close to the grave site.

She should have expected the attention. Her dad was a famous serial killer, after all.

Finally, one by one, they gave up and left, and Christy had a little time alone. The funeral director stood respectfully at the far corner of the canopy with his back to her.

"Christy?"

The voice was little more than a whisper and yet she jumped.

"Sorry." Reilly stepped up beside her, dripping wet. He was in a dark raincoat, for all the good it did, since the left sleeve was draped over his bandaged arm. "Didn't mean to scare you."

She was surprised to see him. She hadn't talked to him since that awful day over a week ago when the EMTs had whisked her off to the emergency room. Reilly had still been in surgery when Ryker's fiancée Nicole had picked her up at the hospital and driven her by Reilly's condo to get her clothes, and then to a hotel.

The next day, she'd gone by Reilly's hospital room, but he'd been asleep.

She hadn't tried to wake him up—hadn't wanted to. She'd just stood at the door and watched him for a while.

His face had been so pale, even against the white hospital sheets. Every so often, he'd winced and his brow had wrinkled. It had hurt her to see him so helpless, so vulnerable, so—human.

But not as much as when Dagewood's bullet had torn into the flesh of his shoulder. The blast, the impact, the blood spatter. The bullet that had ripped into his flesh, had ripped her heart into pieces.

After standing beside her in silence for a few minutes, Reilly spoke. "I'm sorry about your dad."

"Are you?" she asked.

She felt Reilly withdraw slightly, and immediately she regretted her words. There was no reason to be mean to him. He'd almost died protecting her.

But at the moment, she had very little control over not only her words, but her thoughts and even her feelings. She'd thought she was ready for her father's death. She'd even thought it would be a relief, and maybe, in a way, it was.

But her dad's death was also the end of her family. Mother, sister, now father. There was no one left but her. As if to emphasize that fact, the creak of the lever that was lowering her father's coffin into the grave stopped and a metallic thud echoed from the hole. It had hit bottom. She cringed.

"Why don't we go," Reilly said as the echo faded.

She nodded, still not taking her eyes off the grave. She stepped forward and looked down at the coffin. "Goodbye Daddy," she whispered. "I hope you can rest easy now."

She didn't allow herself to think about angels and devils, or heaven and hell. She chose to believe that he was in a place of peace, with her mother and Autumn, and was no longer suffering, either physically or mentally.

Reilly's right hand slipped into her left, and he tugged gently. She let him guide her away from the grave site and onto the path that led to the road. He gave a nod to the funeral director as he led her to a waiting taxi.

The driver opened the rear door for her. She climbed in and Reilly climbed in beside her. The driver got in the driver's seat and pulled out into the road.

Christy sat there with Reilly's right arm against her left.

His lean, strong bulk beside her was at once comforting and disturbing. Neither one was necessarily a bad thing.

"Sorry," Reilly said gently. "I'm soaking wet."

"So am I," she said, and allowed herself to lean slightly into him. She could feel his warmth even through the wet clothes. Dear God, how was she going to live without him?

She closed her eyes, willing herself not to think like that. She'd known from the beginning that any relationship they might have was doomed. He was a cop. Hadn't she had enough trouble with cops in her life? If ever there were two people who could never be together, it was she and Reilly.

"I see you got your pink cast cut off."

She looked down at the wrist guard on her right wrist. "Yes, I did." She flexed her fingers. "It's not completely healed yet, but it will be soon."

Reilly nodded without speaking.

After a moment, Christy looked out the car window. "Where are we going?"

"To my parents' house. They're having an anniversary party. The whole family gets together."

"No, please. I can't. Just take me to my hotel," she said. "Then you can go."

Reilly shook his head. "No. You have to go with me. My mother sent me after you."

She couldn't. She just couldn't deal with meeting strangers. Not today of all days.

Reilly turned toward her and she heard a barely audible gasp. "Oh, Reilly. I didn't ask how you are. You're hurting."

"A little. But I'm fine. I'll be out for a few weeks, until this damn shoulder heals, and it feels like somebody launched a cannon into the middle of my chest, but I'm fine." He paused. "I wanted to check on you, but by the time I could, you were gone."

She nodded. "I had to go back to Boston to arrange for

leave. I thought—" She swallowed. "I went to ask for more time to care for Daddy."

Reilly's hand covered hers. She pulled it away. "Reilly, please take me to my hotel. I appreciate your mother's invitation, but I don't feel like talking to strangers."

"They're not strangers. They're family."

"Right. To you. They're your family. Not mine." She winced at the harsh tone of her voice and resisted the urge to put her hand against her throat. She'd sounded so—mean.

"They could be."

Christy was sure she'd heard him wrong. "What?"

"They could be," he repeated.

She turned to look at him. Those intense, ridiculously blue eyes were on her, but for the first time since she'd known him, they weren't sparkling with confidence. They were wide and full of something she couldn't quite put a name to. Doubt? Apprehension? *Fear?*

"I don't—" she said, not even sure what she was protesting. "I can't—"

"Can't what?" His eyes changed then. Not that the apprehension was gone exactly. But something darker, something dangerous broke through. The brilliant, clear blue of his irises seemed to turn a deep navy and his brows lowered.

"Can't what, Christy?" he demanded.

She swallowed. "You're—you're a cop."

"Yeah? So what?"

She moved away from him—not far, as the backseat of the taxi wasn't that big. He grasped her hand again, not allowing her to break contact.

"So *what?*"

"I can't—I don't—"

"You can't trust a cop. Is that it?" Now his eyes were blazing. "After all that's happened to your family, there's no way, right?"

She opened her mouth but nothing came out. His vehemence was scaring her. She'd only seen him like this once before, but then, his anger hadn't been directed at her. Now it was. Distractedly, she noticed that the taxi had taken a turn then come to a stop.

"If that's what you really think, then fine. I'll send you on your way back to your hotel. But first, I want you to think about something." He stopped and closed his eyes for a few seconds.

She couldn't help but study his face. The skin over his cheekbones and temples was drawn and his lips were tight at the corners. He was exhausted and in pain. And it was her fault. "Reilly, don't—"

"Shut up, please," he said quietly without opening his eyes. "I need you to listen to me for just a minute."

She waited.

He finally opened his eyes. "You do trust me, Christy. You may not realize it, but you've trusted me ever since you first spoke to me at the courthouse. And not once have I betrayed your trust. Not once."

Christy frowned at him.

He watched her carefully, then leaned his head back against the headrest and closed his eyes again. "Just think about it."

"Reilly?" she said, but he didn't answer. She put her hand on his forehead. He was hot, and his skin was damp with sweat. The flesh beneath his eyes looked faintly bruised.

He was wrong about her trusting him. Wasn't he? Hadn't she been wary of him ever since she'd found out he was Detective Ryker Delancey's twin brother?

After all, Ryker had arrested her father and put him in jail, where he'd had a heart attack. How could she trust him *or* his identical twin brother?

But Reilly had been there for her every single time she'd

needed him. From her attack at the Oak Grove Inn to the moment she'd been taken hostage by Jazzy and Detective Dagewood.

He'd declared himself her knight in shining armor, and that's exactly what he was. Tears welled in her eyes and slipped past her lids to slide down her cheeks.

"You're right, Reilly," she whispered brokenly. Her fingers still stroked his forehead. "You've kept me safe from the very first moment we met. I owe my life to you."

"You don't *owe* me anything," he muttered without moving. "That's not what this is about."

She swallowed. *Mama, Daddy, Autumn—help me.* "My mother was killed by a policeman. My sister was killed by a detective. My father—" Her voice broke, so she stopped. With each word she said, Reilly's face grew more grim, his lips tighter.

After a moment she continued, "But for what it's worth, and whether my family…approves or not, I'm in love with a cop. A cop who's been my knight in shining armor from the moment I first laid eyes on him."

To her surprise, Reilly's pinched lips relaxed and spread in a little smile. He caught her hand in his and brought it to his lips. When he opened his eyes, Christy gasped at the impact of his gaze. "I've loved you since I watched you walk across the marble floor of the courthouse, Doc. I've just been waiting for you to realize you love me."

"You could have just told me," she said and laughed, even though tears were still streaming down her face.

Reilly shook his head and then pulled her to him and kissed her. "No," he murmured against her lips. "You had to figure it out yourself."

Somewhere in the middle of a longer, deeper kiss, Christy heard the taxi driver clear his throat.

Reilly pulled away. "Okay," he said. "Are you ready to meet your family?"

The words tumbled from his lips without effort. But to Christy they sounded alien. "My family," she said hesitantly, testing the words.

Reilly nodded. "They can be, if you let them."

She looked out the hazy windows of the taxi. They were parked in a long driveway that curved in front of a huge brick mansion. White columns spanning three stories and at least four balconies ran along the front and around to the sides of the huge house. There were more than a dozen cars parked in the driveway.

"How—" Christy swallowed. "How big is your family?" she managed.

"Not as big as I want it to be," he said. "I want babies."

She looked at him in surprise. "You do?"

"Sure. Why do you think I'm asking a pediatrician to marry me? I figure if anybody's good with kids—"

Her breath caught. "Oh, Reilly!"

"Okay, wait. Before you get all mushy, I need to tell you the real reason I want you to marry me. I'd really like to beat Ryker at one thing. He's planning on getting married in June. How about we have a Christmas wedding?"

"You want to marry me so you can beat your twin brother?" she asked, unable to keep a smile off her face.

Reilly shrugged, then winced. "Well, among other reasons," he said. "Do you think you'd be willing to marry a cop?"

"As long as it's the right cop," she answered, leaning over to kiss him.

The taxi driver cleared his throat again, but the knight in shining armor and his damsel, no longer in distress, didn't hear him.

* * * * *

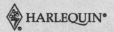 **HARLEQUIN**

INTRIGUE

COMING NEXT MONTH

Available December 7, 2010

REQUEST YOUR FREE BOOKS!

2 FREE NOVELS PLUS 2 FREE GIFTS!

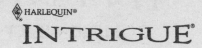

♦ HARLEQUIN®
INTRIGUE®

Breathtaking Romantic Suspense

HARLEQUIN®

A Romance

FOR EVERY MOOD™

Spotlight on

Classic

Quintessential, modern love stories
that are romance at its finest.

See the next page
to enjoy a sneak peek from
the Harlequin® Romance series.

*See below for a sneak peek from our classic
Harlequin® Romance® line.*

Introducing DADDY BY CHRISTMAS by Patricia Thayer.

MIA caught sight of Jarrett when he walked into the open
lobby. It was hard not to notice the man. In a charcoal
business suit with a crisp white shirt and striped tie covered
by a dark trench coat, he looked more Wall Street than
small-town Colorado.

Mia couldn't blame him for keeping his distance. He
was probably tired of taking care of her.

Besides, why would a man like Jarrett McKane be
interested in her? Why would he want to take on a woman
expecting a baby? Yet he'd done so many things for her.
He'd been there when she'd needed him most. How could
she not care about a man like that?

Heart pounding in her ears, she walked up behind him.
Jarrett turned to face her. "Did you get enough sleep last
night?"

"Yes, thanks to you," she said, wondering if he'd thought
about their kiss. Her gaze went to his mouth, then she
quickly glanced away. "And thank you for not bringing up
my meltdown."

Jarrett couldn't stop looking at Mia. Blue was definitely
her color, bringing out the richness of her eyes.

"What meltdown?" he said, trying hard to focus on what
she was saying. "You were just exhausted from lack of
sleep and worried about your baby."

He couldn't help remembering how, during the night,
he'd kept going in to watch her sleep. How strange was
that? "I hope you got enough rest."

She nodded. "Plenty. And you're a good neighbor for

coming to my rescue."

He tensed. Neighbor? *What neighbor kisses you like I did?* "That's me, just the full-service landlord," he said, trying to keep the sarcasm out of his voice. He started to leave, but she put her hand on his arm.

"Jarrett, what I meant was you went beyond helping me." Her eyes searched his face. "I've asked far too much of you."

"Did you hear me complain?"

She shook her head. "You should. I feel like I've taken advantage."

"Like I said, I haven't minded."

"And I'm grateful for everything…"

Grasping her hand on his arm, Jarrett leaned forward. The memory of last night's kiss had him aching for another. "I didn't do it for your gratitude, Mia."

Gorgeous tycoon Jarrett McKane has never believed in Christmas—but he can't help being drawn to soon-to-be-mom Mia Saunders! Christmases past were spent alone…and now Jarrett may just have a fairy-tale ending for all his Christmases future!

Available December 2010, only from Harlequin® Romance®.